Winter Symphony

OVERTURES - BOOK ONE

*A Mature Couples,
Second-Chance
Musical Holiday Romance*

By Jean Maxwell

Dedication

For R.
My first.
My last.
My Imzadi.

Foreword

Enjoy a complimentary eBook from this Author when you join the Jean Maxwell Community!

Sign up at idreamofjean.com and be first to hear about upcoming releases, giveaways and exclusive content.

Prologue

April, twenty years in the past

"I have to go." She groped for her wristwatch on the night table, where thin light from a bedside lamp cast long shadows across the small room.

"You could stay," he said.

She sighed and shook her head. "You know I can't. It would take a lot of explaining."

He lay against the pillows with his hands tucked behind his head, his tousled, dark bangs draping diagonally across his forehead. His lips curled in a wry smile. "So what? You're good at that. Stay."

She flashed him a look that said, 'don't tempt me,' as she lifted her body and swung off the bed, her pussy slick and wet from their lovemaking. She grabbed her panties from the pile of clothing on the floor and slipped them on. A warm sliver of cum began to trail down her inner thigh. "It's late," she whispered, reaching for her shirt and jeans. "I shouldn't have stayed even this long."

He rolled onto his side and watched her as she donned her clothes. "Always unfinished business with you," he said, his hazel eyes still full of mischief. "Was it good for you?"

She tucked her shirt into her jeans and sat on the edge of the bed. "What do you think? Of course it was. It was my idea, remember?"

He nodded and reached out to grasp a lock of her long blond hair. He let his hand trail the length of it, stroking it to the ends then starting at the top again. "Yes it was. I hope you're not in trouble. In any way."

She turned to face him. "Like I said. It was my idea. And I'm on the pill, if that's what you're referring to." She wrinkled her nose and let out a low chuckle. "Hell of a time to ask."

"Yeah. I guess," he said, and laughed along with her. "So let's do it again." He tugged on her hair playfully. "And again, and again."

She loved the sound of his laughter, his voice in whispered tones, and the sight of his naked body lounging casually on the bed. She loved everything about this man, she always had. So many years spent dreaming about this moment, just these few hours alone and aware; where nothing existed except the two of them.

And now it was over.

"Shhhh," she scolded. "That's enough." She leaned down and kissed him lightly on the lips. "I know the way out."

She left the apartment and stepped out into the warm spring night. Her car sat parked on the curb outside the building. Glow from the streetlights filtered into the vehicle and reflected off the long white box that lay in the back seat next to her flute case. It held the wedding dress she'd picked up from the seamstress on her way to rehearsal earlier that evening. It represented hundreds of dollars of satin and lace and almost as many hours of stitching and fitting.

It represented reality.

The path forward.

The road not taken.

She swallowed hard and slid behind the wheel, knowing she'd just done the hardest thing she'd ever do; spoken the most calculated lie she'd ever tell.

And drove away.

Chapter One

November - present day

Jenna Layton-Brophy pulled into her driveway. At the push of a button, the garage door began its slow mechanical rise. As it retracted on its rails, it revealed the rear end of a muddied Sequoia SUV.

He's home already.

The realization registered in her brain with mixed feelings. On one hand, she should be glad that her life partner had arrived home early, and safe. On the other hand, inevitably the one that played devil's advocate, it made her wary. *On your toes, sister, figure out what's to be the problem of the week and prepare your defense.*

Apprehension swelled in her chest. What had she left un-done that would become the opening salvo for today's continuing battle? Dirty dishes in the sink? Pool chemicals left unbalanced? Perhaps neither, perhaps both; and she was beginning not to care.

She eased her Lexus ES into the garage alongside the Sequoia. Engine off, keys out. She retrieved her flute case from the back seat. With the Winter Symphony concert rehearsals starting tomorrow, she'd had the tech shop check it over and replace the pads. She passed through the connecting door to the interior of the house. The boys were still at school and the hallway quiet. From upstairs, she heard the shower running and exhaled in relief; thankful for a few moments reprieve before having to face him. *Stupid.* Surely she had nothing to fear from a partner of nearly twenty-two years. That's what most people would believe. *What did they know.*

She busied herself loading soiled dishes from the counter into the dishwasher. Maybe Matt hadn't seen them yet; if so, she still had time for a pre-emptive strike on the unfinished tasks from this morning. Not that it mattered. It never seemed to make a difference how much or how little Jenna did around the house. The one detail she missed would always be the topic of criticism.

Jenna opened the fridge and sifted through the jumble of items inside, seeking long-forgotten leftovers or empty jars to purge. Soon, Matt's footsteps pounded down the staircase.

"I see you made housekeeping a priority again," he said as he entered the room, sarcasm thinly concealed beneath a calm voice.

Jenna whirled to look at him, feigning surprise. "You're home early. Job shut down because of the snow?" she asked, changing the subject to avoid the inevitable argument that hung over his words like a brewing storm.

Matthew Brophy stared at his wife for a moment, seeming to consider whether he thought she was either stupid or deaf. "Yeah. Site too wet to pour the concrete today." His wind-burned jaw needed a shave and his pale blue eyes, hooded with age, bored at her from within their hollowed depths. "I'm tired as hell. Think I'll take a nap. You planning on starting dinner anytime soon?"

"It's only four o'clock," Jenna replied. "Plenty of time. Or are you in a hurry?" His needling condescension irritated her to the core. It seemed to rear itself at every opportunity lately, more than usual. Or did she just notice more than usual? Either way, it grated.

Matt chose not to answer. He grabbed a beer from the refrigerator and left the kitchen in favor of his more popular destination, their large sectional sofa in the living room. It gave a squeak as he flopped upon it. The can's pull-tab hissed, and the television blared to life with a click of the remote.

How was your day dear? How's the orchestra sounding? When's your concert, I'd really like to go to it. These were statements Jenna knew she would never hear from her husband's mouth. Instead, there would be comments about how dirty the floor looked, or had she remembered to make this or that appointment, or picked up groceries. My God, hadn't she always done these things? Did he have to ask? They'd been married too long for this kind of uncertainty. Surely they were past this kind of antagonism. It was like living with one's boss, having to issue a progress report every day.

Jenna searched her memory for some shred of a time it hadn't seemed that way. She'd loved Matt; she married him, raised two children. Their relationship hadn't always been easy, but why had it seemed to get harder as the years went by? It made no sense, no logic.

"By the way," Matt's voice grumbled from the other room. "I'm taking that fly-in job starting next week. It's a 14 and 7 shift right through Christmas."

Jenna stopped what she was doing and chewed her lip for a moment, willing her anxiety down before responding. "We talked about that. I thought you said you were going to turn it down."

"We need the cash," he said.

Another jibe at Jenna's inadequacy. Her own salary apparently didn't figure into his assessment of their financial situation. Worse, he placed no importance on being home during the Christmas season, leaving her to do all the shopping and preparations--and of course, be unable to attend her concert. In all the years they'd known each other, he could never seem to remember when she had a performance date coming up, or even what days of the week she had rehearsal.

In the past, while the boys were growing up and they were a struggling young family, Matt often had to work out of town for long periods. Not unusual in the construction industry, but it had been years since he'd needed to do that, their financial picture having improved considerably, enough to buy the three thousand square foot house they now lived in, and two luxury vehicles to boot.

She shook her head. A 14 and 7 shift meant fourteen straight days working then seven off, and rotating that way for the duration of the project. Which could be weeks or months, one never knew for sure.

Jenna slammed her hand on the counter. The fact he'd changed his mind without consulting her hurt the most, and she felt something snap inside. She wanted things to change, and change now. Her feet propelled her into the living room.

"What are you talking about?" she demanded. "We don't need the cash. We've got two paychecks coming in. Why would you want to be away during Christmas?" Jenna's outburst startled Matt from his near-doze and his head jerked up at the sound. His opened beer sat untouched on the coffee table.

"Hey," he barked. "Don't you shout at me. What's up your ass?"

"What's up my ass?" she mimicked. "What do you think? First you say you're not taking the job, then you accept it without talking to me. On top of that, you're taking off on us right when we should be spending time together as a family."

Matt scowled, looking like a bear woken too soon from hibernation. "Well somebody's got to pay the bills around here.

It sure as hell isn't you," he said, bitterness layered on every word.

Jenna's blood surged in her ears. His criticism of her earning power had been uttered one too many times. With a shaking hand, she picked up the beer can. "Is that so? Maybe a few less of these would make the budget easier to manage!" In the next second, the can flew through the air between them and landed against Matt's chest, its contents spraying and foaming in all directions, soaking both his shirt and the coffee table.

Matt bolted upright, batting the can away to spill onto the carpet as well. "You're crazy!" he spat.

Jenna let it all go. All the hurt, all the pain and neglect she'd felt but never vocalized rushed to the surface in one uncontrollable wave. "Me, crazy?" she shouted, her eyes widening in anger and her skin burning in the familiar, sickening way it did when she knew she'd gone too far; stepped across a threshold that offered no retreat. "Is it crazy to want one decent kiss in twenty-two years? Crazy to hope that at the end of the day someone has a little something left for the other people in his life besides TV and a can of beer?"

He stood and moved past her into the kitchen, turning his back on her. Jenna followed, her tirade fueled to the next level. "You know what? You're boring. You're the most boring, unpleasant person I can think of. Not one good thing to say about anyone or anything; and you know what's worse? Other boring people I can walk away from. But you plant your boringness in the middle of the room like an elephant. Too big to step around, too small-minded to communicate with."

Matt wiped at his shirt with a dishcloth. He didn't look at her, didn't speak. He didn't appear to even hear her words or be aware of her presence. He threw the soaked cloth into the stainless steel sink and disappeared into the garage. The Sequoia's engine rumbled to life.

Jenna didn't wait to watch him leave. She spun and ran upstairs to the bedroom they shared, closing the door and leaning on it while her body shook with rage and despair. Now she'd done it. They'd argued before, but this time a line had been crossed. Part of her felt sorry, and part did not. Which would come out the stronger?

Despite her momentary courage in finally speaking her mind, she didn't feel strong at all. On the contrary, she felt weak and dizzy. As her trembling knees gave way, she collapsed onto the king-sized bed and cried.

Chapter Two

A white blanket of new snow covered the pavement and sidewalks of the city. With each miserable step, Jenna's boots poked black holes in its serene surface as she hurried along 97th street to the backstage doors. Slipping inside, she brushed the heavy, wet flakes off her instrument case and the shoulders of her coat. A round-faced security officer nodded and grinned at her from behind his wall of glass. "Hi Martin," she said, with a cheerfulness she did not feel inside.

Jenna made her way to the dressing room to doff her winter gear before heading to the stage. Many other members of her group, the Edmonton North Shore Orchestra, had already arrived, including Jenna's long-time friend and fellow flutist, Heather Harris.

Jenna gazed at the scene, women fixing their hair and makeup after coming in from the snowy outdoors, assembling their instruments and shuffling sheet music in preparation for the rehearsal. The holiday season had begun, and she decided that even arguing with Matt wouldn't dampen her Christmas mood. She resolved to rejoice inside, reaffirm to herself her luck in having the greatest job in the world.

Being paid to rehearse and perform music year-round described a dream come true for Jenna. She came from a musical family, and took up the flute at a young age; but hadn't played professionally until the opportunity to audition with the North Shore Orchestra came along. Though her fiftieth birthday had come and gone, the knowledge that music would always be part of her life gave her strength of purpose.

Flute in hand, Jenna left the dressing room for the rehearsal stage. Heather followed behind her. "Are you looking forward to the Winter Symphony?" Heather asked.

"Yeah." Jenna replied. "A nice change from the usual Christmas concert, don't you think?"

Heather nodded. "Should be a fun program," she said. "Except for that one piece." She threw Jenna a cross-eyed look that left no doubt as to which one she meant.

Jenna laughed. "Oh, that one has its' moments. I don't mind it."

"Sure, you at least have a nice solo in it."

"You want it?" Jenna asked with an innocent smile.

Heather made a face and shook her head from side to side. "Noooo thank you." They took their respective seats and began to play long warm-up tones while the other orchestra members gradually filled the stage.

North Shore's Director, the illustrious Winston May, had announced the Winter Symphony concept to the group in September. He'd described it as "a modern musical theatre celebration of the Christmas season". The ambitious, multi-movement work consisted mostly of new compositions but also contemporary arrangements and variations on themes of traditional carols. They expected a sold-out house.

Jenna and Heather continued their warm-up among the usual organized chaos of 40-plus musicians milling about, adjusting their chairs and music stands in preparation for the day's rehearsal. Jenna leafed through the pieces in her folder, finding her solo part to run through one more time, even though she'd rehearsed it plenty at home.

Immersing herself in her music banished the sting of Matt's hurtful words. Outright quarrels like yesterday were infrequent, but he always seemed ready to criticize her at any other time. On one occasion he'd actually said: *"I get more action from the on-demand adult channel than from you. Go ahead, run off to rehearsal and collect your piddly little paycheck."* After twenty years of marriage, he still did not understand her, nor wanted to try. He couldn't see past his own needs, plebeian as they were. In two sentences, he'd demeaned both her sexual and financial worth. What sort of man does that?

She worked over a difficult passage, playing the notes in tempo first, then again more slowly. She memorized the finger positions in sequence and repeated the passage several times, working up to speed.

Movement in the wings caught her eye. Their manager Ruby Smythe stood talking with someone in the partial shadows offstage. Everyone loved Ruby; a super-organized, dedicated woman that ran the administrative side of things for the orchestra. She approached the podium.

Her countenance serious as she stepped up to face the musicians, she held up one hand. Someone from the back row whistled a call to attention. Jenna's curiosity rose; Ruby rarely addressed the group unless it was of logistical importance.

"Hi everyone," Ruby said, adjusting her glasses and placing both hands flat on the podium. "There's been a change of plans for the concert. For those of you who may not know, Winston has been called away due to a family emergency. I understand his mother is gravely ill, and he's gone back to England to be with her until further notice." Gasps of shock and concern rippled through the crowd.

"Mrs. May is quite elderly," Ruby continued, "and we just don't know what the outcome might be. Winston thought it best to not plan to conduct the Winter Symphony." She glanced around the stage, allowing a moment for the musicians' reaction. Murmurs and whispers of concern fluttered about the space. "He sends his apologies, and has arranged for a replacement. I think you all know him, so please welcome, from Vancouver, Mr. Brandon Marsh."

The group applauded as Mr. Marsh entered from offstage. Ruby retreated, also applauding, to let him take the podium.

Jenna's heart clenched at the sound of his name. She stared in shocked silence as he strode to the front of the stage, smiling and tossing a casual wave to the crowd. Standing just shy of six feet tall, he wore jeans and running shoes. She noted the well-developed shoulder muscles underneath his white crew-neck sweater, and thought he appeared amazingly trim and athletic for a man in his fifties. While sporting more than a few wisps of gray, his hair remained as dark, full and wavy as she remembered it—falling across his forehead as he lay there in bed, asking her to stay.

"Hi guys," he said. His voice sounded very informal, as expected. He was one of them.

He'd lived here, attended high school here, and played principal trumpet in this very group before moving to Vancouver to assume that role on a bigger stage. He'd done very well for himself on the gray and rainy west coast since then. Now he stood barely a metre away from her, making her pulse race and her breath accelerate.

"Let's start with the Overture," he said, arranging his scores on the podium. He picked up the baton, and began directing the group. Jenna focused on the music, following Brandon's movements while counting measures of rests until her entrance. He was a capable conductor, and appeared to be enjoying every minute of it. Jenna listened to the other sections of the orchestra, 'seeing' the music in her mind, feeling the melodic pulse throughout her body. She swayed slightly to the beat, her count flowing mentally, carrying body and soul along with it.

Three two three four, Four two three four. She raised her flute to her lips anticipating her entrance at measure six. Five two three four, breathe in. Downbeat on six. Attack. Her notes rang clear and strong, the captured air unleashed into the instrument and flowing steadily through to the end of the phrase. *Nailed it.*

They were all part of the whole, every player on the stage completely in the moment, the result greater than the sum of the individuals. All of them shared the same passion and reason for being here, to experience the soul-satisfying rush of melody and countermelody culminating in pure and fearless sound. It made her feel alive more than anything else in the world, and helped wash away any sad, cruel or painful truths that dared to intrude on her joy.

When the rehearsal ended, several people swarmed around Brandon, asking how he'd been, catching up on old news. Jenna gathered up her music and retreated to the dressing room as quickly as possible. She wasn't about to stand in line for him.

She disassembled her instrument into its case. If Brandon Marsh would be conducting the Winter Symphony, she would be seeing plenty of him over the next several weeks. There was no hurry, and certainly no need to hover around him in admiration and awe like the others. A lot of water had gone under the bridge in twenty years.

But that hadn't stopped the feelings. A voice echoed in her mind. *"Always unfinished business with you."*

She hadn't seen or spoken to Brandon since he'd quit North Shore and left the city all those years ago, but their story didn't start there. It began in the back row of a high school band room. She could practically smell the aging carpet, the stale insides of a rented instrument case, cork grease and valve oil. Memories flashed in her mind of a shared wink in the hallways, dancing in a darkened gym, and kisses in the back seat of a car.

From the day she'd laid eyes on Brandon Marsh, Jenna had been smitten. There was no other word for it. Suddenly, on the first day of her senior year, there he was; the handsome and talented trumpet player, wearing a brilliant smile and the mysterious allure that went with being the new kid just moved into town. She'd been drawn to him like oxygen to a fire.

They dated that entire year, and she recalled with aching clarity all the heady new feelings and experiences that went along with it, the kind only teenagers can fully appreciate. She adored him, but the more Jenna thought about those days, a hollow pit formed in her stomach. In spite of that giddy, adolescent romance, and an unspoken but stubbornly lingering attraction in the years since, Brandon never chose her.

He'd received a scholarship to the prestigious music program at Northwestern, and left for the States right after graduation. She heard from him less and less as his four years ticked away, but nothing prepared Jenna for what happened when he returned.

Brandon got married.

To some girl he'd met at the University named Nina. *Who the fuck was she?*

Hurt, confused and angry, Jenna turned away, forced him out of her mind and carried on with her life. She completed her own studies in both art and music, got a job, auditioned for North Shore and earned her chair.

She'd moved on just as Brandon had; but as the saying went, karma's a bitch. Brandon's marriage fell apart; and just as he and Nina were breaking up, Jenna became engaged to Matt Brophy. Worse, Brandon got the nod as principal trumpet for North Shore at the same time. She winced at the irony. For a pair of trained musicians, their timing really sucked.

She endured sidelong glances and polite interaction with Brandon at weekly rehearsals, hiding her feelings deep inside, until that night. A few days before her wedding, something inside Jenna urged her to make a move, or regret it forever. They'd been just high school kids, barely understanding their sexuality when they'd first met; she didn't want to live the rest of her life without knowing how it would feel to truly *be* with Brandon on an adult level of intimacy. She'd never get another chance.

She asked him to bed with her and he accepted. They made love in his apartment. Wonderful, unselfish, cognizant love that they knew would have to last them a lifetime. Though filed away for two decades, the memory of that night still haunted her, as she hoped it haunted him. In its way, it was an act of finality; the closing of a book that perhaps neither of them truly wanted to close.

Jolting herself back to the present, Jenna gathered her music and instrument and headed out the way she had come in. Re-living old fantasies didn't change reality. As she crossed the length of the hallway and turned left toward the backstage exit, a voice called from behind her.

"Hey, where do you think you're going in such a hurry?"

Jenna whirled around and saw him. Even after twenty years Brandon looked as handsome as ever, gray hairs and laugh lines notwithstanding.

"Hey!" she said brightly, hoping she didn't look overly awestruck to see him. "Look at you, Maestro. How've you been?" She took a step toward him, a warm smile on her face. After all, they were still friends.

He held his arms wide. "Not even a hug for an old bandmate?"

"Of course," she said, moving into his casual embrace. His arms felt good around her, however loose and non-committal they might be.

"You're looking well," he said as they stepped apart again.

"Thanks, but don't look too close," she replied. "Likewise, you look terrific. Life on the coast seems to agree with you."

His hazel eyes glittered back at her. "Thanks. Life on the coast is wet and miserable most of the time," he said. "But I'll take that as a compliment."

She swatted him on the shoulder. "Yes, it's a compliment. So, how do you think the rehearsal went? You seemed to be enjoying yourself. I like your conducting style."

"It's going to be a great show. You played well. But then, you always were a strong player."

"Ah thank you, thank-you-very-much," Jenna replied in her best mock Elvis. Brandon laughed. "Are you staying in town until the concert?" she asked.

"Well, that's still weeks away. I'll probably stick around until Friday, then back to Vancouver for the weekend."

Jenna nodded, acknowledging an illogical sense of disappointment. She saw some other musicians approaching from the rehearsal room, and wanted to wrap it up while she still had his full attention. "Well, it's really great to see you, Brand," she said, pressing one hand to his chest. "Gotta go. But we'll see you next rehearsal, right?" She stepped backwards in the direction of the exit.

"Right," he agreed. "See you then." He continued to smile and stare at her, as if amused she was trying to run away. It wasn't altogether untrue. She certainly felt like running away—from unhappy thoughts and her troubled marriage;

from a dangerous, unfulfilled longing that stubbornly refused to dim with the passage of time. From secrets and lies.

With a wave, Jenna turned and left the concert hall.

Chapter Three

The next morning not only Jenna's brain awoke, but something else within her. A sense of being alive in a way she hadn't before. She'd come to a fork in the road of her life and veered left instead of right. There'd be no going back.

For two nights now, Matt hadn't come home. Not a call nor a text. Fear had taken its place among the mix of her emotions. No matter the schism between them, Matt's absence had the same effect as a floor dropping out from under her. She felt unbalanced, shaky. Her actions had been rash, no question. Was she really prepared to live without him? Were the boys? They knew nothing yet; and she wasn't about to tell them anything until she herself understood what would happen next.

The cold light of day didn't always make you see things more clearly.

She had been married for nearly a quarter century, and, with the exception of Matt, for most of that time never concerned herself if any man she happened across was handsome or plain, or what he might be like in bed. For a long time, she would look away during the love scenes in a movie. She supposed she had spent so long as a mom that nearly every romantic impulse had been stomped out of her. On the other hand, it was difficult to feel romantic toward someone who, she had to say it, was a fucking grouch most of the time.

She was proud of her two sons, Taylor and Kyle though. In their late teens now, they were handsome and popular, both skilled athletes. It had been a bit heartbreaking for Jenna when each of her boys reached about eighth grade, and she realized she would not have the same kind of mother-child relationship with them any longer. They were becoming young men, feeling the tug of their own hormones and voicing their opinions with increasing volume and decreasing tact.

When the girlfriends began appearing, any thoughts of her sons having intimate relationships sent her into a swirling fog of denial. But lately she saw them in a new light; realizing how mature they were becoming, and that sooner or later they would break away from their parents.

Adding to the matter, the sight of Brandon Marsh striding into her life again had roused the sleeping goddess within her. Twenty years evaporated in a heartbeat, and she felt desire deep in her belly for the first time in what seemed like forever.

It occurred to her that her children were now the same ages as she and Brandon when they first met. This seemed a weird juxtaposition; she couldn't imagine any of Taylor's girlfriends making such an impression on him that they would still be in touch two decades from now. How could they possibly have any serious connection at that age? Had she felt like she knew her own mind back then? Been completely aware of her feelings for Brandon, and that they went a lot deeper than most? *Oh yes.* She could admit that much.

She forced herself out of bed and into the shower. As she toweled off, she caught her reflection in the huge bathroom mirror. Funny. She hadn't looked, really looked, at herself in a long time. Suddenly the idea of Brandon seeing her naked form made her panic. She peered critically into the polished glass.

The mirror could be lying. *Please let it be lying.* Jenna turned sideways and craned her neck to get an angle on her backside. Her ass had always been her best feature. Now it sported several dimples and…oh dear, sagged a little? *God.* A few sets of squats each day might cure it. And the nagging little pouches of flesh above the bra line...rowing machine, would that fix it?

She turned to face front, her wet hair draping in strands over her breasts and trickling water down her abdomen. While the ass may have gone south, the boobs seemed to have marched to the front battle lines. A decent bra created cleavage for the first time in her life. Not fair. Why did nature see fit to rile up her hormones at this stage of the game?

Jenna shoved these thoughts aside and got dressed. A dreary Wednesday loomed ahead with worry over Matt, gray skies overhead, and worst of all, no rehearsal until tomorrow. Brandon Marsh would have to remain a dream for one more day. She went to the kitchen and readied breakfast for Taylor and Kyle.

"Morning, Mom," their soft voices echoed as they shuffled into the kitchen a little after eight o'clock. "Mmmm, cinnamon toast!" Jenna smiled. It didn't take much to please these two; breakfast generally alternated between cinnamon toast, instant oatmeal and frozen waffles.

They sipped tea and crunched down toast together. Neither of the boys asked about their dad. Normally, he would have left for work by now anyway. She gazed across the table at nineteen year-old Taylor, her firstborn. His dark brown, wavy hair dipped over his brow line as he leaned forward, concentrating on his plate. Sixteen-year-old Kyle's lighter, sandy-blond bangs shaped into an upflip that framed his face and his striking blue eyes. Taylor's sturdy frame contrasted with his younger brother's slim and tall one. They finished their breakfast and rose from the table.

"Thanks, Mom," Taylor said as he donned his jacket and dug a set of car keys from the pocket. "Kyle, get your shit and let's go."

"Yeah, I'm coming," Kyle grumbled, taking his plate and mug to the sink. "See ya later, Mom."

"Bye, guys. Drive safe, Tay." Jenna cleared the table, grateful that they could get to school on their own and her days of chauffeuring were over. It gave her time to think, to reconnect with her own interests and ambitions after so many years of structuring her life around them. Today, however, that concept seemed a little sad.

She waved her sons goodbye as they drove away in Taylor's sporty little truck that they'd bought the year before. The vehicle had been yet another bone of contention between her and Matt, but it didn't matter anymore. From the moment she'd woken this morning, Jenna knew her time as Matt's wife had come to an end.

She spent the rest of the morning in her 'music room,' an upstairs bonus room typical of the style of homes in the neighborhood. She assembled her flute and began to play. Each note of the Winter Symphony score made her think more and more about Brandon. It seemed crazy to expect there might still be a spark there. The fact he was conducting the orchestra for the next several weeks was purely coincidental. Nothing could be prophetic or fateful about it, she reasoned; but that didn't clear him from her mind.

The music filled her, consumed her, for the next two hours. And while the Christmas melodies brought joy, they also brought memories. At the end of her session, she realized how terribly lonely one could be, even when surrounded by family.

She thought about her last private moments with Brandon, all those years ago, and a flame ignited deep within her; the memory of the touch of a man who truly lit her fire. Suddenly her body ached with desire, and she retreated to the bedroom as though trying to hide from herself, and what she wanted to do next.

It didn't work.

She undressed herself and lay down. To hell with self-control. She spread her legs and reached down, caressing her inner thighs with both hands. Fuck, it seemed ages since she'd enjoyed orgasm; and it looked like it would be up to her to change that. Her fingers twined into the hair covering her mound. She wondered if that were strange these days, keeping hair on her pussy. Many salons offered Brazilian waxing; did men like that? Hairless pussies?

She had no frame of reference; she'd only been with one man for many years and he'd never expressed an opinion either way.

Jenna rubbed herself, easing her labia apart and nudging the wet tissues between. Her hips jerked with sudden arousal, a warm tingle spreading like fire across her abdomen and the muscles of her inner thighs. She wanted to be wetter yet; stroking the length of her canal she dipped a finger into her vagina, gathering slick fluid from inside and spreading it onto her exposed genitals. Her fingertip grazed the sensitive edge of her vulva as she withdrew her finger, sending ripples of pleasure through her core. Damn, she was ready to come, even with these light touches. If there were a big, stiff cock in the room she'd want that inside her now, thrusting mightily and pushing deep. She didn't even own a dildo, or even a vibrator for that matter. The idea hadn't occurred to her before now.

She settled into a rhythm of pulses that triggered more moisture; her fingers pummeled her swelling clit, making tiny smacking noises. The sound lit her imagination, picturing Brandon's face near to hers, and his hands doing the touching. *"Do you like this?"* she imagined him whispering. *"Do I make you feel good? That's it, baby, let me make you feel good…"*

She began to pant, her breath quickening and moans escaping her lips. "Yes, baby…don't stop baby….oh, God…! Jenna's voice hurled the words into the empty air of the bedroom, and surrendered to the sensation, the blissful waves of climax that washed over her like a rushing tide. "Brandon…"

Her entire being vibrated and thrummed for those precious seconds, riding out the swells of pleasure as they peaked and dimmed, and felt the afterblush of tiny contractions in her private muscles, until the sensations ceased altogether.

She lay there with eyes squeezed shut. The silence of the room became palpable, growing in intensity as though the silence in itself made sound, underscoring just how alone she truly felt. A stinging sensation built behind her eyelids, and her hands, having done their work, slid around herself in a protective hug. She turned her face into the pillow and let the tears flow like the notes from her flute.

Chapter Four

Jenna awoke with a chill, startled to discover herself lying naked on her bed. She hadn't meant to cry herself back to sleep. The draft from the windows made her shiver and she reached for the fleece throw at her feet to cover herself. *What time is it? Are the boys home from school? Shit! I should be starting dinner.* These immediate thoughts rang loudest in her mind, but as she rolled to her side, hugging the soft blanket closer around her she thought about sex.

Mom masturbating in her room…jeez. How cliché was that? Did she enjoy it? *Hell yes.* Did she wish she weren't alone? *Damn straight.* She felt caught somewhere between shame and satisfaction. She hoped that wouldn't be the limit of her future sexual gratification; lying here alone and fantasizing about a man who could never be hers.

And what of the man she already had? To whom she'd vowed to love "until death parts us." She could still remember the reverend's words from their wedding ceremony so long ago. How could anyone possibly live up to that expectation? To say that 'people never change' was a lie; or at least an untruth. It seemed to her that a person's negative traits, though inherently always present, just amplified over the years. It certainly worked that way for Matt. His self-centered nature had been evident early on but Jenna had been willing to overlook this for the sake of home and family.

One thing became clear. She couldn't stay in the same house with Matt after this. She felt the need to clear out before he returned home, get some headspace to figure things out. Unless he'd already made that decision, and wasn't coming home at all. Jenna sighed and rose from the bed, still clutching the blanket. Where could she go, and how? An idea occurred to her, and as she dressed, she thought it through. The cabin at Whiteridge. They sometimes rented it in the winter months, but for the most part spent summers there in years gone by.

Rehearsal would finish Thursday afternoon. She could leave on Saturday morning, and be there by noon. She realized she'd need to stay and face Matt, ask to borrow the Sequoia for the trip as the mountain roads might be treacherous now. She wouldn't trust the lower-slung Lexus if the weather worsened and the snow got too deep. She went downstairs to start dinner and find the number for the reservations office.

*

The house still felt cold despite the oven's heat as it simmered a beef roast. The boys watched TV while Jenna tossed the salad and set the table. A few minutes later she heard the garage door lurch open with a grinding of gears. Matt had decided to come home after all.

They ate dinner in silence, Jenna trying to keep bits of conversation going, but without much success. Taylor and Kyle soon excused themselves, and Matt took his plate into the kitchen. Jenna followed behind and approached him as he stood at the sink with his back to her. "I won't ask where you were the last two days. But I think we need some space from each other," she began. A few moments of silence followed with no reaction or response from him. She stared at the back of his head, his once-thick blond hair shaved close not only because of his work, but as his preferred method of disguising his growing bald spot. "I'm going to go up to the cabin at Whiteridge for the weekend, and maybe a few extra days. Stay out of your way until you're ready to leave for the job. Is that okay with you?"

Matt shoved his dinner plate into the dishwasher with enough force that the growing row of dishes clattered against one another. "Do what you want. Why ask me?" he said.

"Well, I need to borrow the Sequoia. Taylor can get you to the airport in his truck. I'm leaving Saturday morning."

Matt remained facing away from her. "Don't pretend like I've ever had any authority in this house. You just do what you want anyway."

Jenna's back rose. "I do not," she replied, straining to keep her voice low. "Nobody has authority over anybody. You're the one who makes decisions without discussing them first. I'm at least being upfront about it."

"I'm gone on Tuesday. You can have the house to yourself after that. Why bother renting the cabin? That's stupid."

So much for pragmatism. Why did she even try to get through to him? Waste of bloody time. "No," Jenna said. "I have to leave now."

Matt turned to look at her for what seemed like the first time in weeks. He eyed her with suspicion. "Why?"

"Because this is over. I can't live with you anymore. And I don't want to."

"Is that so," he sneered, nodding his head in contempt. "Now who's making decisions without asking? He gave a derisive snort. "Go on, take the Sequoia; go to the cabin. But you'd better be the one paying for it. And don't think you'll be welcomed back with open arms."

Jenna's vision misted over in a curtain of red. How dare he play the "if you leave don't bother coming back" card. That illustrated just how little he thought of her and the 20 plus years of her life she'd committed to this relationship. She let silence take effect and returned his icy glare before turning an about face and leaving the room. He'd find out. It was 20 years of his own life he was tossing away, too.

*

Another dump of snow greeted rehearsal day. After a fitful night spent sleeping in the spare room, Jenna dressed without much thought, feeling too drained to expend further energy on deciding what to wear.

At breakfast she told Taylor and Kyle about her plans for the cabin. "You guys gonna be okay getting to school and back for a few days without me?"

Taylor threw her a look. "Mom. We've been doing it ourselves for more than a year already. We can handle it," he said, his tone a mix of humor and exasperation. Kyle remained silent, preferring to carve into his syrup-laden toaster waffles. "Is something going on between you and Dad?" Taylor asked.

Jenna's lips tightened, knowing the question would eventually come, but not having prepared a satisfactory answer. She exhaled a resigned breath. "Maybe that says it best," she replied. "There's absolutely nothing going on between me and your dad." She paused. "Absolutely nothing." She searched Taylor's eyes for comprehension. "Do you understand what I mean?"

Taylor nodded slightly. "I knew for awhile. You guys are breaking up." He shrugged. "It happens."

Kyle swallowed a mouthful of waffle and looked over at the two of them. "Shit happens. We're not dumb, you know, Mom. We see what's going on."

Jenna wavered between laughing and crying. Her boys were so sharp; and so grown up. Why hadn't she noticed?

"No." she agreed. "You certainly aren't dumb." She moved to their side of the table and gave them each a hug. "You're brilliant."

*

Jenna entered the dressing room at the concert hall with less spring in her step than usual. In spite of her excitement over the Winter Symphony programme, not only her feet seemed heavy but her soul as well.

After a lackluster practice session, the whole orchestra seemed as down as she. Seated on a tall stool at the front of the group, Brandon seemed to sense the gray vibe in the room. "Okay," he said, sliding his baton into its leather case. "I think we need a break. Let's come back in twenty."

The musicians dispersed, most in search of coffee or water or wandering off to check their cell phones. Jenna's stomach twisted as she rose from her chair and made her way to the water cooler. Stress and lack of sleep had taken its toll. As she sipped a paper cup full of water, she felt a hand on her arm.

"Hey." She turned to see Brandon at her elbow. "You okay? It's not like you to blow a solo. Something wrong? Can I help?"

"Just tired," she said, managing a weak smile. His presence warmed her spirits a little, but she felt nervous around him when not feeling her best. She didn't want him to see her listless or vulnerable, and for heaven's sake not with bags under her eyes from a sleepless night. She withdrew from his touch. Damn, all this time wanting to be close to him and she found herself backing away.

"That's all? You sure?"

She nodded, and he released her arm.

"Hmmm. Not sure I buy that," he said. "How about some lunch and a drink when we're finished here?"

Jenna blinked. She had no reason to think that lunch would be anything other than platonic and casual, but something in his voice said otherwise. "That sounds great. I'd love to, thank you." The words tumbled from her lips without effort, without hesitation.

Brandon smiled and gave a curt nod. "See ya then." He walked away just as quickly as he'd appeared.

*

A table by the window afforded a great view of the snowy, downtown cityscape. They waited for their drinks to arrive, a tea and amaretto shot for Jenna, a rye and diet coke for Brandon. Jenna admired the view, not quite sure how to start the conversation. Brandon saved her the trouble.

"So how have you been, really? It's been a long time."

Jenna smiled. "Yeah, it really has." She looked at him directly, indulging herself in a close inspection of his face. He didn't look all that different, she concluded. Or was she seeing him through the rose-colored glasses of youth? It didn't matter. Brandon, her first love, would look the same to her whether sixteen or sixty. His hazel eyes with adorably long eyelashes. Infectious smile. The swath of dark hair that brushed sideways across his forehead and partially hid the vertical scar on it that he'd told her was the result of a coffee table crash at the age of five.

"You haven't changed at all," he continued. "I don't see even one wrinkle."

Jenna smirked. "Oh, there's a wrinkle or two, trust me." Their drinks arrived, and she began steeping the teabag in its little pot and pouring half the amaretto into the tall mug. Neither of them spoke. Where do you start a conversation that's a rehash of the last twenty years? "So, you were put squarely into a dad role when you moved away," she said. Through the music grapevine, she knew he'd married a second time, wife number two having come complete with tween-aged children. "How was that experience for you?" Even as she asked the question, her insides twisted.

"It was an eye opener." Brandon stirred his cocktail and looked up at her with a half-smile.

"I'll bet," she said. "Kids were certainly an eye-opener for me. But lucky you, you got to miss out on the bottle and diaper stage."

"Not to mention childbirth," he added. "But Trish had a routine down with the kids way before I came along. I didn't have a lot to do; and they spent time with their natural father quite a bit, too. He didn't take kindly to 'stepdad' being in the picture."

"How old are they now, are they still living at home?" Jenna asked.

"At home? Naw, Jason lives in res at the University, and Mandy moved in with her boyfriend two years ago. I'm an empty-nester at the age of 53."

Jenna laughed at the irony. It wasn't really even his nest, truth be told. In a way, Brandon had always gotten the fast track to things without paying the dues that went with them. "Really? That must be nice – do you travel, make love on the kitchen table, that sort of thing?"

Brandon raised an eyebrow at her. "With my rusty joints, I can barely sit at the kitchen table these days, never mind make love. The body just ain't what it used to be, honey. And I haven't really had time to travel, other than music conventions and tours. You?"

Jenna sipped her tea. "Well, yes I have travelled a bit, not that we could afford it. But we did it anyway. A lot of nice trips," she affirmed, thinking about some of them. "But I get what you're saying. It's a bitch when you're betrayed by your own body, isn't it? Aches and pains, joints that squeak, not being able to get up or down off a chair without making a noise of some kind. Brutal."

Brandon laughed and took a drink from his highball glass. He looked thoughtfully out the window into the gray skies. "Did you ever think we'd be here discussing this stuff at our age, Jen?"

She smiled and shook her head. "No. Weird, isn't it?" She felt anxious, unsure how much longer she could hold back what she wanted to say to him. Speak the words that had been brewing in her mind. "Brand," she said, taking a deep breath. "I've been thinking about something. When you get to a certain age, you realize that life is short, and you're too old to beat around the bush anymore. You have to say what you mean, wouldn't you agree?"

He turned his head slightly and threw her a curious gaze. "Okay…yeah? And?"

Jenna swallowed. No time to be coy. She must look him in the eyes for what came next. "I want to see you," she said, searching for a reaction in his face. He stared her down, waiting for more. "I want you to know, I'm not going through a crisis, or looking for sympathy or advice, or anything like that." He nodded slightly, encouraging her to continue. "But I do want you to know, if you didn't already, that even after twenty years, marriages and children notwithstanding, I've been in love with you since I was sixteen. That my heart flips over anytime your name is spoken, or when you walk in a room. And I still want to jump your bones. I want you to go to your grave with this knowledge. Do you understand?"

Brandon pressed his lips together, thinking. "Yes," he finally said. "I can't deny there's always been something between us. We wouldn't be sitting here talking if there weren't."

Jenna exhaled. The hard part was over. What would he think about her next words? "I'm going up to the mountains this weekend. I've rented a cabin at a resort up there. Would you meet me there, spend the night?"

Brandon looked puzzled, and kept his silence for a few moments. Jenna steeled herself for whatever words he would say next, no matter how much they stung.

"Where is your husband?" he said calmly.

Jenna blinked. Of course he would ask this. Brandon always said what needed to be said, when the chips were down. She had a feeling he didn't mean Matt's physical whereabouts. After a long pause, she answered. "In a place neither of us can come back from."

Chapter Five

Roschkov Professional Corp displayed on the Blackberry screen. Brandon cursed. He'd hoped for at least a few days' reprieve before hearing from Roschkov the Ruminant. No such luck. "Brandon Marsh," he answered.

"Hallo, Brandon." Roschkov's heavy Slavic accent pierced through the wireless connection. "Is dis a goot time?"

Good as any, Brandon thought, lowering himself into the hotel room's lone armchair. The words "What's up, doc," came to mind, but instead he replied with, "Of course, go ahead."

"How are you feeling, any new symptoms?" the doctor asked.

"Nothing notable," Brandon said, feeling irritated for no particular reason. He hurried the conversation. "I'm in

Edmonton now, working with the North Shore Orchestra. I assume you have the test results?"

"I have them back from the lab. The good news is that growth is slowing from the last set of tests. You seem to be responding to the supplements. But it would be wise to begin a drug treatment as well."

No. No drugs. Not yet. "I think I'd like to just stay with the palmetto and lycopene a while longer," he said, after a brief silence. "I don't plan to be back in Vancouver for a few weeks. I couldn't start any new treatment until then."

Dr. Roschkov sighed. "I see. I suppose it can wait, but I caution you, these things are best treated early. Make sure to call Irina and make an appointment for when you return."

Brandon doodled on a notepad with the hotel pen, its' ballpoint scratching deeper into the paper as he applied more pressure, inking in the patterned shapes he had drawn. "Yes, I'll do that."

He disconnected the call. Roschkov. The Urologist from Ursk and his nurse, Irina the Impossible. He pictured the doctor in his mind, munching every imaginable kind of vegetable from a plate on his desk. Roschkov the Ruminant. He ate more greens than any goat. Maybe that's why the old geezer had lived so long. In retrospect, wouldn't have been a bad example to follow. Roschkov wasn't the one potentially diagnosed with prostate cancer. *Dammit.* Just as Jenna had said, life was so short; and dictated only by the choices you made along the way.

Seeing her again reminded him all too clearly of his choices. He should have known a self-centered girl like Nina was all show and no substance; that she would never have been happy living in 'the sticks' as she so often called Edmonton, waiting for the big break in her singing career that never came. Still, he chose to fall victim to her pretty face and flattering words; chose to ignore all the red flags, and chose to marry her in spite of them. It came as no surprise that she discarded him like a chart in a bad key, and left him for another man just a few years into their doomed union.

However, what had surprised him were the strong feelings Jenna had evoked in him over the last few days; glowing to life again like the embers of a fire that had never been completely put out. It wasn't the first time she'd offered him such a bold invitation, and it stirred up many fond and vivid memories of the last occasion she'd done so. He'd never forgotten it, or her. There remained unfinished business between them even after all these years.

Brandon sighed, the weight of regret hunching his shoulders. He didn't know how many choices he had left; but whatever the number, he decided he wouldn't waste a single one.

*

Jenna packed her bags absentmindedly. Her brain just wasn't firing on all cylinders. Normally a trip to Whiteridge involved either skiing or hiking, but this week was an exception. Brandon hadn't given a firm answer to her invitation to join her at the cabin. He'd thanked her, but said he would have to think about it and let her know. They exchanged cell phone numbers and said goodbye at the concert hall.

She threw random pairs of underwear, socks and bras into her suitcase. A few sweaters, jeans and fleece leggings followed. Just as she zipped the bag closed, Taylor appeared at her bedroom door.

"Take your stuff down to the car, Mom?" he asked. Jenna nodded. As he grasped the handle and hoisted the suitcase into the air with one muscled arm, he seemed to sense her apprehension. "Cheer up, Mom. It'll be good for you to get away. Wish I could go; the ski hills will be open soon."

"Yeah, probably," she agreed. But you've got school. And you're right, a change of scenery will be good." She followed him down stairs and out to the garage. After a hug and kiss for each of her sons, she started the big SUV's engine and drove away.

On a crisp December day with overcast skies, the roads were clear as she left the city. Three hours of driving, and a steady climb to higher altitudes met with colder air. As she neared the turnoff to Whiteridge, it began to snow. Heavy flakes gathered on the windshield, and Jenna was glad to have chosen the Sequoia for the trip. Soon the familiar sign indicating the turn to Whiteridge appeared, and she steered the vehicle off the main road and uphill along a narrower, less traveled route. No tracks except her own marred the snow-covered trail.

In another ten kilometers, Jenna breathed a sigh of relief as she rounded the last curve and passed through the rustic wooden gates of Whiteridge. She came to a stop outside the main lodge and threw the gearshift into park. The circle of twelve cabins stood silent and pristine on the hillside above with their steep-pitched gable roofs ensconced in fresh snow. The tennis and basketball court looked lonely and abandoned for the winter. The last time she'd stood here, her life wasn't poised on the brink of the unknown. Her place in the order of things had been firmly established as a wife and mom.

After checking in, she made her way up the inclined drive to cabin eleven. The snowfall had tapered to a lazy drifting of tiny flakes that collected on top of the exterior lanterns and the quaint little holly wreaths that the management had taken the trouble to affix to each door.

Inside, everything looked pretty much as she remembered. The small anteroom with its wooden ski rack and coat hooks led to the main room with its weathered plank floor and braided scatter rugs. The flagstone fireplace dominated the space, its chimney drawing the eye upward to reveal the cozy loft bedroom above.

She nudged the thermostat up a notch, and began to unpack her supplies. A rustic maple table and chairs adorned the kitchen nook, and she filled the matching maple-front cupboards with cans and packaged food. A small refrigerator was just large enough for the fruit, vegetables, milk and soft drinks she'd brought. She set a bottle of whisky and two bottles of wine on the counter.

She gazed around the room again, noticing the pine-paneled walls had been painted white instead of varnished in their natural color. The three-seater sofa in front of the fireplace had been re-upholstered. On the hearth lay a small faux-fur rug; a new addition to the décor. A narrow bookshelf stocked with paperbacks and magazines filled the corner to the left of the fireplace. A metal floor lamp with a kooky lampshade sporting moose and pine tree silhouettes stood on the right.

Beyond that was a short flight of open-tread stairs that led to the loft. Jenna grabbed the rest of her gear and climbed up. The bed looked very inviting with fluffy pillows encased in crisp white linens. A down-filled comforter and patterned throw cushions made her want to flop onto its campy softness. A dresser, nightstand and blanket box completed the furniture ensemble. The pitched roof came to a peak in the center of the room. A lovely octagonal window just beneath the peak spilled wintry light into the space.

The furnace had begun to warm the whole cabin, and lent an aura of peace around Jenna as she unpacked and laid her things into the dresser drawers. If Brandon didn't show up, she'd at least get lots of practice time. When she finished, she set her flute case and music folder on top of the dresser. She wasn't really in the mood to play right now. She descended the stairs and opened one of the bottles of wine. Picking a random book from the shelf, she curled up on the couch with a glass of red and a fleece blanket, and began to read.

Her eyes grew tired as the room darkened with the falling dusk. Her neck felt a little sore, too. She snapped the book closed and went to switch on the hideous moose lamp. As the bulb came to life, so did the whole lamp. The shade began to turn, like a jewelry box ballerina, creating a rotating circus show of moose then forest, then moose again. Jenna laughed. The rusty gears made a grinding noise as they spun the sad hinterland parade.

The buzzing of her cell phone interrupted her laughter. She thumbed the screen to answer the call.

"Jenna? Hi. It's Brandon. If the invitation's still open, I'm coming up."

Chapter Six

"Park by the tennis courts," she told him. "I'll come get you there."

The last four hours seemed the longest ever, waiting for Brandon to arrive at Whiteridge. She'd cautioned him not to come until the next day, even though the waiting was hell. At last, around mid-afternoon he'd called when he made the final turn into the gates. She disconnected and pulled on her coat. The day had dawned with more heavy snowfall, making the road up the hill from the main lodge nearly impassable for anything but a four-wheel drive. Plus, the cabin's driveway had only space for one vehicle; all other guests had to park down by the main lodge. The Sequoia's engine roared to life, and she backed out of the lone parking stall.

Her windshield wipers swished aside the growing layer of snowflakes as she drove down the hill to meet him. Turning into the main parking lot, she spotted Brandon's Acura facing the tennis court. Drifts of snow piled up against the wire fence both inside and outside of the court. She pulled alongside the Acura and pushed the button for the automatic window on the passenger side. Brandon did the same.

Pellets of snow whipped in diagonal lines between them. He gave her a warm smile; a knowing smile. It made Jenna think of a beloved farm animal, knowing it was being led to slaughter, yet completely trusting in its master. "Hi," he said.

"Welcome to Whiteridge," she said, returning his smile. "Valet service, sir?"

"You bet," he said, hitting the close button for the driver's window again. "This snow is crazy."

Jenna hit the power lock switch for the doors. Brandon retrieved a duffel bag and instrument case from the back seat of the Acura and pulled open the passenger door of the Sequoia. "This cab for hire?" he joked.

"Sure thing, buddy. Where to?"

He placed the bags in the rear seat and climbed in. "To hell. Or heaven, I'm not sure which. Maybe both. And step on it."

Jenna grinned and threw the gearshift in reverse. *It might be heaven, but I'll give you a hell of a ride there,* she promised herself. "Any trouble finding the place?" she asked, looking out the rearview, trying to calm herself in his presence. It had never been easy, and she felt as giddy as her sixteen-year-old self again.

"The turnoff was well marked. Didn't expect the road conditions though. What sort of place have you lured me into? Kinda off the beaten track, wouldn't you say?"

"I'd say more like perfect." She felt her cheeks burning as she grinned even more widely. She glanced sideways at him. He looked out the window as they drove, observing the snow-laden spruce that bordered the narrow road.

"Perfect," he echoed.

"We can pick up firewood here," she said slowing at the top of the road where a metal lean-to sheltered neatly split bundles of birch. "Would you mind?"

"Not at all," he said, already opening the vehicle door. She watched him grab a bundle in each hand and step around to the back of the Sequoia. She hit a button and the rear hatch floated noiselessly open. Damn, these new SUVs were slick. Clunk, clunk, as the bundles hit the cargo floor. Brandon closed the hatch and hurried back into the passenger seat. Snow had settled on his hair and shoulders.

"Thanks," she said, and moved the vehicle forward again toward cabin eleven. She realized that number eleven stood furthermost into the woods from the ring of other cabins in this loop. Subconscious Freudian decision? Maybe. She drew to a halt, and put the SUV in park. "Here we are."

Brandon nodded. "Here we are. Wait a sec," he said, getting out. He walked to the driver's side and opened the door.

Jenna laughed. No one had opened a door for her in a long time. It felt both sweet and pathetic.

He carried the wood bundles along with his duffel and case as she led him inside. She hung his coat next to hers near the old ski rack. "Make yourself at home," she said, gesturing to the couch.

He looked around the place. "Nice," he said. "I can get that fire started for you."

"Okay. Kindling's in the basket there," she said, pointing to the fireplace. I'll make you a drink in the meantime. Wine, or a rye coke?"

He smiled and tilted his head toward her. "You even have to ask?"

Jenna chuckled and nodded. "Rye coke it is," she said, and moved to the kitchen to mix it. She took in all the sounds around her, the clink of ice cubes against glass, the strips of wood being stacked against each other, the strike of a match. She wanted to remember everything about this moment. She smelled a hint of sulfur as the match blazed alight; inhaled the oaked vapor of the whisky as she poured. It occurred to her that she hadn't even thought to bring a CD player or an iPod, or even a radio. How ironic; for two people to whom music meant so much, they would have nothing to listen to. But he'd brought his trumpet; maybe they could play a duet.

She turned and watched Brandon as he crouched on the hearth with his back to her. He nurtured the small flames ablaze by adding one careful piece of wood at a time, building a pyramid of sticks that allowed the needed oxygen to enter beneath. She crossed the room and bent down next to him.

"We have ignition?" she commented, handing him his glass.

He glanced at her sideways. "I think so," he said. His fingers rested against hers as he took the glass from her. "But it might need some fresh air."

"Plenty of that up here," she replied.

His hazel eyes met hers straight on. "Sure is." He took a sip of his drink, then turned to the fireplace, blowing a jet of air into the tent of sticks. The flames shot up in response, consuming the slim tinder with crackling speed.

Jenna smiled, and held out her free hand. "Come and sit." He took it. They moved to the big couch and sat down to admire the growing pyre. "I'm so glad you came. I wasn't sure you would."

Brandon sat silent for several moments. "I wasn't sure myself. But...certain things made themselves clear to me in the last few days." He sipped his drink and gazed into the fire. "Other things, not so much. I guess I'm still wondering what's going on in your life. And your head. Do you make a habit of cheating on your husband?"

"God, no," Jenna said, taken aback. "I could ask the same of you. Do you make a habit of cheating on your wife?"

"No," he said quietly. "Tell me what's going on."

She took a deep breath. "It's over. I don't know what snapped exactly, but I just know I can't live that life anymore.

Can't live with him, any more. We're just…planets apart. I should have seen it long ago. He doesn't care about me, about what's important to me. I mean nothing to him."

"That can't be true," Brandon said. "Maybe it's just your perception. Don't throw things away so easily. Not like I did."

"You mean with Nina?"

"Partly. I mean, you should focus on what you've got, not what you haven't got."

Jenna scowled. "I plan to focus on what I want, not what I've never had."

Brandon drained his glass in one final gulp. "I see."

"Another?" Jenna asked.

"Why not," he answered.

She took both their glasses and mixed another two rye and cokes. It occurred to her that they should probably eat something, if they were going to keep drinking. The notion dismissed itself as ice cubes splashed into the dark liquid. Eating could wait. She returned to the couch with drinks in hand, watching as he added a few split logs to the fire. "Here's to what we've got," she said, offering him his drink and raising hers in a toast.

Brandon stood and took his glass from her. "And what have we got?" he asked, a smile tugging at one corner of his mouth.

She sat down, looking up at the flickering firelight reflecting in his eyes. "We've got tonight. We've got this place, this privacy. Let's make the most of it. There's a bed upstairs."

"I'm not here to take advantage of you. You're in an emotional state; are you sure that's what you want?"

"I told you what I wanted at lunch the other day. I'm not looking through a cloud; in fact I think I've never seen more clearly. I want to be with you, Brand. Is that so hard to understand?"

He gazed back at her, his expression amused but cautious. "No. I guess I'm just surprised."

"Surprised? What, that I would be so forward? That I would still want you after all these years? I never stopped wanting you, Brandon. It may be crazy, but it's true."

He shook his head, his expression turning apologetic. "No, I believe you. I think I'm more surprised at myself. I should know better than to open old wounds."

Chapter Seven

"What do you mean, old wounds?" Jenna laughed. "Yours or mine?"

Brandon looked away into the flames, the crackle and snap of the fire the only sounds around them. It seemed even the fire mocked him, the sounds punctuating the anguish he felt. He should tell her everything, he knew he should. He wanted it all to come out now. Life was indeed too short, just as she'd said. All that wasted time. "I just don't want either of us to have any regrets."

Jenna inhaled a long breath then let it out. "Neither do I. If you truly have no desire to do this, if it makes you uncomfortable or you feel there's too much at risk, then we won't. I won't ever speak of it again."

He stayed silent for several moments. He didn't mean to be evasive, but wanted to be sure she wasn't just on the rebound, or trying to get revenge on her husband. "I'm not with Trish anymore. I'm on my own again," he said quietly.

Jenna didn't respond immediately. She swallowed with difficulty, as though her mouth had gone dry. "I didn't know. Seriously, Brand. I didn't know. That's not why I invited you here, to pounce on you while you were vulnerable."

Brandon made a sniffing noise. "Didn't you?" He knocked back his drink and set it aside. He sat down next to her and leaned forward, elbows on his knees. He looked at her face, outlined by the glowing flames. The sun had set in the past hour, and except for the fire, the room lay in darkness. "We never contacted each other for years. Why else would you start this, now, unless you knew something had changed?"

"Something did change. I changed," Jenna confirmed. "I had no idea you would turn up on the podium at North Shore; and I had no reason to think your situation was any different than ever. But when I saw you I realized…I needed to be with you. I hoped you would want to be with me. Just for awhile. No strings."

Brandon chuckled at her choice of words. "Is that a pun?"

She let out a low snicker in response. "No, Maestro. I meant no strings attached."

They knew each other so well. They could find humor even in the darkest corners of their lives. The fire continued to pop and hiss, the moisture steaming out from the frozen logs he'd piled in it. "The answer is yes. Yes, I want to do this with you. We should have done it a long time ago."

"We did do it, a long time ago," she reminded him. "In your apartment, after rehearsal. And you told me then, you wanted to do it again."

Now it was his turn to laugh. "I didn't think it would be twenty years later," he said.

"I knew what you meant," she affirmed. "But I was getting married in a few days. Too little, too late. What you didn't know is how my heart leapt when you said it."

"It seems our timing has always been a little off, hasn't it?" he admitted.

Jenna clucked her tongue. "Now that really is a pun. And the understatement of the century."

Brandon nodded silently, rubbing his hands together.

"Look, for whatever reasons, we were never together for real," Jenna continued. "I never asked you point blank why, that's one of my mistakes. And I don't need to know. I've made my peace with it. All I really needed to know, was that if I reached out to you now, would you respond. And you did. That's all I need. And here we are. Please, Brand, let's just give each other this gift."

"You're wrong. There's so much more you need to know," he whispered, his voice barely audible. "You have a lot to lose, too. Why would you take this risk?"

"It's over between Matt and me. What do I lose?" she leaned forward, her face close to his. She tilted her head slightly, as if signalling him to think about it. "My career is established. I've raised my kids. RSPs are in the bank. There's really not much I can screw up at this stage. If I get a divorce, Matt would still end up paying. You know that better than anyone." She reached out and covered his hands with hers. "What I would lose, is this chance for true joy. And so would you."

He brought her hands up to his mouth. He considered his next words carefully, as he always did. "Do you not feel anything for your husband? Nothing?"

Jenna looked a little disturbed at this question. "Listen to me," she began. "I've been a faithful wife for twenty years. I gave. He took. I had some mean things said and done to me, and I've put it behind me. I fulfilled my commitment. It's my time now. To do what I need, what I love, what fills my heart with joy."

"The commitment was 'til death do us part,' as I recall," he countered.

She blinked and drew back slightly. "Really? I don't see either Nina or Trish lying six feet under, pal."

Touché. He let it go for now. If Jenna was right, if she was being truthful, what she proposed was magical. The human capacity for love was truly extraordinary. Where did it say things had to be all or nothing? You could love your spouse, your children, your parents. Loving any of them didn't diminish your feelings for the others. But one needed the love back. Like everything in life, there were wants, and there were needs. If the wants are not satisfied you are disappointed, but if the needs are not satisfied—you die. It was very simple. He understood now; they were both dying in their own ways.

Jenna raised her hands, pushed his shoulders back so that he reclined on the couch with his head lying on the armrest. She tossed the back cushions onto the floor, then leaned in close. Her lips grazed his in the gentlest of touches. The smell of wood smoke wafted across to them, the flames' warmth heating their skin.

Staring into his eyes, she whispered, "I'm gonna rock your world so hard." Her voice trailed off as she pressed her lips firmly to his. He could see the flickering firelight reflected in her pupils, dilated in the dark of the cabin. He knew he wouldn't say no to her; not now, not ever.

He returned her kiss gently at first, but within seconds their lips recognized each other with full clarity of who they were, where they had been, and where they were going. Their tongues explored each other's mouths, hungrily giving in to sensation and desire. She began undoing the buttons on his shirt. Brandon let himself relax, allowing her to proceed as she wished. This was her show, her composition. *Let her take the baton*, he thought. She slipped her hand inside his shirt, caressing his chest as though re-acquainting herself with his body.

Breaking their kiss, Jenna pushed herself upright, straddling him while finishing off the buttons, pulling the shirt tails out from his jeans and stroking the full length of his torso with both hands. She took her time, admiring what she saw, touching his warm skin, his chest hairs sliding between her fingers. He watched her face, with the mysterious smile on it. He could feel the rush of blood making its way to his loins, right about where she was sitting on him. *Thank God, everything's still in working order. Roschkov had cautioned him that sex might be a problem with his condition.*

It seemed she could feel it too and her hands stopped moving over him. She reached for her own shirt, slowly undoing the buttons, but never breaking eye contact with him. The shirt peeled away, revealing a lacy black bra that accentuated the contoured fullness of her breasts.

Brandon bit his lip, thinking how lovely she had remained over the long-lost years; and at the same time feeling those years rewind.

She reached for the front clasp of the bra, twisting it open and baring herself just for him. Pert nipples stood at attention amid the dark circles of her areola, in contrast to the arc of firelight reflecting on the curves of her round breasts. She dropped the bra to the floor, and began to work on his jean buttons. His erection was rock-hard now, something he'd avoided since the doctor's warnings. He reached up and took her breasts in both hands, feeling their weight, brushing the rough nipples with his thumbs as they tensed with arousal. She leaned down to him, and he slipped his arms behind her back, pulling her close, and with a twist of his body rolled them both onto the floor.

She shrieked in surprise as they landed with a soft thump on top of the cushions. He took her breasts into his mouth, alternately licking, sucking and biting on the nipples, and working on undoing her jeans with one hand. Jenna arched her back, breathing heavily, eager to wriggle free of her pants, and pushing on his waistband at the same time.

When they had rid themselves of their clothing, their hands roved over one another as if in a quick review of each other's physical landscape. Not unlike the way they would have studied a long-forgotten music manuscript.

Jenna stroked Brandon's thighs, working her way towards his hard cock. She stroked it from the front and then the back, around the tip and back again. He could feel his heart pounding, his satisfied moans muffled by her eager lips that fully engaged with his own.

She rolled him onto his back, breaking the kiss and making him look up into her eyes. She winked, then lowered her head down to his chest where her tongue blazed a tantalizing trail from his right nipple down across his stomach. It darted playfully around his navel then traced a line further south, until she could take him fully into her mouth. She glazed his hard muscle up and down with her lips as though she meant to swallow him whole.

Brandon entwined his fingers in her hair, pulling not-so-gently as she worked on him, his cock sliding in and out of her delicious wet mouth. His mind spun, wanting to find release but holding back at the same time, so the pleasure wouldn't end. It felt crazy being here with her—crazy, wild, wonderful. How did this woman pull him so completely into a maelstrom of desire? She'd been schoolmate, lover, friend, colleague, adulteress and a dozen more things to him; been in his life so long he could barely remember a time when she had not.

Jenna let go of him, moved upward to meet him face to face again. She placed a hand on each of his shoulders, pinning him to the floor and drawing her legs up on either side of him. Their eyes locked as she placed herself upon him, slowly, letting him enter her inch by maddening inch, watching him take short gasping breaths inward as he succumbed to her.

She rocked steadily, filling herself with his hardness. Then there was nothing left for him to deny, and he let the rush flow out of him, a smile playing at the corners of his mouth as he did so. Reflexively, he closed his eyes, but along with the euphoria he expected came a searing streak of pain. *Roschkov warned me*, he thought wildly; this was his punishment. He could barely form another coherent thought as the agony mingled with ecstasy. His eyes shot open, met by her smoldering blues. She smiled with satisfaction upon seeing his dilated gaze, assuming to have pleased him completely.

He squeezed his eyes shut until the burning delight had subsided, the last of his fluid pumped into her in fading spasms. He waited to catch his breath from the exertion before speaking; he had a feeling that the pain he'd just experienced was only the merest prelude to his punishment. "We are sooo going to hell," he finally said. He had waited too long to find happiness, he realized. And now he must pay.

Enjoying this book so far?
You can leave a review at
goodreads.com/book/show/38122161

Want to read more by Jean Maxwell?
Visit Jean's official website at

idreamofjean.com

Chapter Eight

They awoke amid the white softness of sheets and comforters in the loft bed. They'd fallen asleep in front of the fireplace, but managed to navigate the narrow stairs and slip into bed at some point during the night.

"Morning," Brandon said, as Jenna opened her eyes to the bright room. He smiled down at her, his body propped up on one elbow.

"Morning," she mumbled back, grinning. "How long have you been awake?"

"Long enough to get hard again looking at your naked body."

"Oh," she said with a chuckle, closing her eyes again. She hoped she wasn't dreaming. Her head felt a little thick with the after-effect of several rye-cokes. In a way it still was a dream, but a waking one. Brandon lay here by her side, in her bed, about to make love to her all over again. The moments of long-denied passion of the night before played in her mind.

"Glad you came?" she asked, opening her eyes again.

"Are you?" he countered, his free hand roving across her abdomen underneath the covers.

"Oh yeah," she sighed, her skin tingling at his touch. His palms glided upward to her breasts, cupping and squeezing gently. Her nipples went hard, sending a shuddering chord through her midsection and reverberating in her crotch. "Most definitely." She squirmed slightly at the sensations building inside. She reached for his cock, confirming his arousal as his stiffening erection bounced against her fingertip. "Let me," she said, curling her fingers around it.

"In a minute," he said. "I want to enjoy how beautiful you look lying in bed next to me."

His wandering hand slipped between her legs and rubbed her mound. "Now you let me." Her clit pulsated in anticipation and moisture flooded her pussy. She spread her legs a bit to allow him access. His fingers parted her labia and pressed against the wet, anxious nub of flesh.

"Ahh," she gasped, sucking in a startled breath. She'd waited a long time for his touch, and the intensity of wanting him rushed over her body in a heated wave. He massaged her throbbing clit, and she spread her legs wider.

"You're so wet, baby," he whispered. "So beautiful and ready. You need this."

She gave a weak nod as his movements accelerated, nudging her clit side to side, then swiping his fingers through the full length of her channel. One finger slipped inside her vagina, thoroughly lubricated with her cream and pumped gently in and out. "Oh yes, baby," she said, her voice nearly a whimper.

"I'm here baby, here to make you feel good," he affirmed, his voice low and confident. Jenna felt a smile curving her lips. His words were so similar to those she'd imagined him saying to her before. "You feel good, yeah?" He returned to manipulating her begging clit.

"Yes, oh yes," she panted, her words coming out in halting bursts. The rush of orgasm began to swell like a wave still far from shore, its roots building deep in her core. He bent his head to her chest. His tongue circled around the stiff peaks of her nipples, the skin of her areola tightening in sweet pain. Nothing in the world compared to these sensations, incredibly heightened by the strong emotions she felt toward him. It had never been this good with her husband. Never. Her body resonated to Brandon's touch, like a bow drawn across the strings of her soul.

His lips closed around her throbbing breast, sucking hard on the swollen nipple. Jenna groaned and arched into him, the sensations in her upper and lower body vying for attention. The wave of climax rushed toward shore, soon to break and flood over her. He again focused on her clit, the rhythm of his fingers increasing, pumping her ready flesh into a frenzied crescendo, crying for release.

The wave crested over her. "Brandon!" Her womb shuddered, the rocking pulses of orgasm gripping her from head to toe. She didn't know if she'd whispered his name or screamed it aloud. But she did know that she'd never loved a man as truly and completely as the one giving her this pleasure right now, nor come so hard in all her life; and that she would never let him get away again.

*

They lay breathless in the pile of twisted bedcovers, the aftershock of their lovemaking holding them still, reveling in the silence and the nearness of each other. Jenna's arms locked around Brandon's neck, her face pressed against the warm pulse under his jaw. She drew in the scent of him, swam in it, felt drunk on it. She promised herself she would remember it forever.

He lifted one of her legs to drape over his hips and gently stroked her thigh and buttocks, his touch light and soothing. "Was it good for you?" he whispered, invoking the shared joke from so long ago.

Jenna chuckled into his warm skin, then lifted her head to reply. "The best. A masterpiece, Maestro." He grinned and gave her a playful spank on her exposed ass. Her private muscles responded with a flinch, ready to take the pleasure all over again.

"You deserve the best," he said, flashing a rueful smile. "But I don't think I deserve you."

She looked at him thoughtfully, traced the curves of his lips with a fingertip. "After that performance, you deserve plenty." She unlocked herself from his embrace and rolled him onto his stomach. "Your turn," she said, and reached for a small bottle on the nightstand.

Jenna straddled him, her still-wet pussy settling over his buttocks. His head turned to one side against the soft pillow. "Mmm, you're sticky," he said with a laugh.

"I'll give you sticky," she said. She poured a handful from the bottle into her palm and slapped it onto his back. His body jerked and he made a muffled squawk as the cool oil met his hot skin. She massaged it in, rubbing it upwards from the center then smoothing it over his shoulder blades and up over his deltoids. She gave the muscles a therapeutic squeeze before moving back down again.

Brandon groaned with satisfaction. "That feels great." He let out three short grunts as she pushed sharply in between his shoulders with both hands. "Why didn't I marry you?" he said in a dreamy voice.

She stopped moving her hands. For a few seconds, she let silence speak for her. "Don't you dare torture me with that," she said in a low tone. "You're the only one who can answer that."

But he didn't. *Shit. Why did I say that?* She wanted to press rewind, start over. She started rubbing again, feeling the smooth oil, now warmed from their bodies, slide between her fingers and his skin. *Please say something.*

"I'm sorry," he said.

"You're sorry." Her voice sounded flat. She stroked his back some more, lacking the purposeful pressure of before. "Yeah, we're all just fucking sorry, aren't we." It didn't come out as anger, more like resignation. *Am I angry at him? I should be. But I can't be.* Again, life was too short. *Don't waste another second.* She slid her hands up to his shoulders again and laid her chest against his back. She turned her head, rested her ear at the nape of his neck and looked out the window. The room was so quiet, she could practically hear him wrestling with his thoughts. She could feel his lungs expanding and collapsing beneath her.

"Jen."

"Yeah."

"I said there were things you needed to know. I never told you why Trish and I broke up."

"No, you didn't," she affirmed. "Does it matter?"

"Yeah it kinda does."

"She didn't run off with another dude, did she? Like Nina did."

The muscles of Brandon's face tensed up, as though wincing in pain. "No. She ran off with another woman. A cellist from the Vancouver Philharmonic, no less."

Jenna no longer felt the rise and fall of his breathing, only the pulsing of her own heart. It beat a silent drum stroke for the twisted song he was singing. She let the words he'd spoken sink in. "Wow. That's harsh," she said.

"It doesn't matter now. I got over it. There's something else I need to tell you."

"What?" *Could there be something worse?*

"There's a possibility I'm going to be diagnosed with cancer. I'm under a doctor's care, and it's been manageable so far. But I've got to start some drug treatment soon."

"Oh my God," Jenna whispered. Silence descended in the room like the snow outside the window. Her lips could find no further words, but her brain screamed *No! No, this was too cruel!* Fate wouldn't take him away again just when there was a chance for them to be happy, would it? She had so much still to tell him.

"Now I'm the one who's sorry," she sighed. "Is there...is there a...prognosis?" It sounded more clinical than intended, but it was better than asking, 'How long do you have to live?'

"How long have I got, you mean?"

His uncanny read between her lines stabbed at her heart. "I didn't say that."

"It's okay," he answered, shrugging his shoulders beneath her as she laid on top of him. "I ask myself the same question every day. The doctor doesn't seem to be addressing that topic; maybe that's a good sign. He thinks the drugs will work."

Jenna lifted her head and kissed the nape of his neck. If kisses could cure, she'd be prepared to pucker up for a lifetime and kiss every square inch of him. Her fingertips slid up his arms, and she mentally logged every curve and bump of muscle, every precious hair on his skin along the way. "But you don't?"

"I don't know. I don't want the drugs, I've refused them up to now, but..."

His unfinished sentence alarmed her. "You refused them? For God's sake, why? This is your life we're talking about... you have to try everything, anything!" Her own voice raised in panic.

He twisted his body so that she rolled off him. He turned onto his side and held her close to his chest, his arms wrapping around her in a comforting hug. Jenna closed her eyes against the tears that threatened to spill. She should be comforting him, not the other way around.

"Don't," he whispered into her ear. "Don't be angry. I didn't tell you to upset you; but I needed you to know."

Chapter Nine

She watched him drive away along the snow-covered road that led down the mountain. Ploughs had been through overnight, and Jenna had no reason to worry that the Acura would see Brandon home safely.

She wondered about his home. If Trish had left him, he must still have his house in Vancouver. She wasn't sure where he'd stayed while rehearsing for the Winter Symphony. And what of her own home? Could she ever go back to living in the same house, lovely as it was, with Matt after this? She worried about the boys. Kyle still had another year and a half of high school. It wouldn't be fair to make him move before graduation.

Misery crept into her soul as she closed the heavy cabin door. The joy she'd felt in Brandon's arms and in his kisses was overshadowed by the knowledge of his illness and her impending return home to an impossible situation.

By the time Jenna had packed up and prepared to leave, the sun had come out. Snowdrifts sparkled in the bright light as she loaded the Sequoia and started the engine. Despite the elevation and the beautiful mountain tableau before her, her spirits were anything but high.

The distinctive sounds of Chicago blared through the car speakers as she made her way down to the main road. Every word of every track brought back memories, each note from the brass section reminding her of Brandon, and a time when all cares and worries remained firmly barricaded behind the walls of a soundproofed high school band room. She'd give anything to have those days back; to reset, to take it from the top and get the whole song right this time.

The drive home seemed both long and all too short as she reached the city limits, crossing an invisible line that defined her return to reality and an uncertain future. The Sequoia seemed to know its own way through the city and to her familiar, upscale neighborhood, easing inside the garage and docking itself like one of those robotic floor sweepers. Grabbing her luggage, Jenna entered the house through the connecting door, unsure of what to expect once inside.

To her surprise, the happy scents of pine and cinnamon greeted her. What the hell? Her men generally couldn't care less about holiday ambience, yet the aura was definitely evident. "Hi Mom!" came excited shouts of two voices in tandem. Kyle and Taylor stood in the kitchen, about to mix some sort of concoction in their Magic Bullet blender as they waved her in.

"Hi," she said, raising an eyebrow in amused suspicion. "What's up with you guys?"

"Want a mocha latte?" Taylor asked. "Bet it was real cold up at the cabin."

"Not too cold. Lots of snow, though. Glad I had the Sequoia. And yes, I'd love a latte. Sounds perfect."

Taylor grinned and pressed the mixer switch. The Bullet ground to life with a deafening whine.

Kyle approached to take her bag from her. "I'll put this in your room, okay?"

Jenna just smiled in response. Kyle scurried off as Taylor brought her a tall mug filled with frothy chocolate goodness. She took the warm cup gratefully. "Okay. This isn't normal. What's the occasion?"

"Come and see," Taylor said, waving her to follow him into the front room. She took a sip of mocha as she did so. "Merry Christmas!" he said, gesturing wide with his arm. She looked up to see their 12-foot artificial tree, fully lit and decorated, standing in its corner flanked by two windows on the adjacent walls. The tiny bulbs seemed to wink at her in silent acknowledgement of her newfound yet bittersweet love.

"Ohh," she sighed, her mouth dropping open. "You did the tree yourselves? It's beautiful!"

Kyle returned from upstairs and all three stood gazing at the tree. "We missed you, Mom. Thought we'd brighten things up for you. We know how you love Christmas."

She nodded. "I do love Christmas. And I love you guys!" She set her cup down and wrapped them both in a group hug. Tears of joy, regret and hope streaked down her face as she let her reserve of the past days crumble away. No more being strong—she didn't need to. Her boys would be her strength. She could do what she must.

She released them and stepped back. She swiped at her wet eyes and stifled a sniffling breath. She looked into Taylor's hazel-brown eyes, now seeing even more clearly the resemblance to his father. Kyle too, his parentage evident in his blue eyes and wiry blond hair. The two roads of her life converged in this pair of men that stood before her. Her love for them told her she hadn't chosen the wrong path; but she hadn't followed the right one either. It was time to explore the road not taken.

*

Brandon hesitated to punch Roschkov's number into his cellphone's keypad. Making the appointment seemed akin to admitting defeat, but the pain he'd experienced at the cabin frightened him. He'd committed to directing the Winter Symphony performance, and if he flew back to Vancouver now, he could be back in a day, two at the outside and only miss one rehearsal before the final dress rehearsal.

The Doc had yet to confirm a diagnosis, but time had now become the most precious resource. If the drugs would buy him that, so be it. He had more to live for than just a concert. Being with Jenna again opened his world like a rare flower—made him see things in high-def Technicolor. How could he not have heeded the signals, seized the moment all those years ago? They'd had the most incredible sex ever, and their time at the cabin only underscored that point.

Unfinished business. He should have never let her leave his apartment that night. He should have carried her to his car and driven off somewhere, anywhere; a thousand miles away from the schmuck who, from the sounds of it, made her little more than his slave for the last twenty years. But he didn't. He'd let her go. Worse, he'd married practically the next woman who walked in his door only to help raise her kids and have her walk right out again. Now who was the schmuck?

"Dr. Roschkov's office." Irina's soft Russian accent filtered across the line.

"Hello, this is Brandon Marsh. Dr. Roschkov wants to see me as soon as possible. I can be in the city tomorrow morning."

"Of course, Mr. Marsh. Is 11:00 a.m. suitable?"

"Fine," he said. After hanging up, he browsed the airline sites to book a morning flight. He was about to dial Ruby Smythe, when an incoming call buzzed on the screen. "Christ," he swore under his breath, then swiped to answer. "What do you want, Trish?"

*

Jenna signed the cheque and handed it over to the resident manager. "Here you are," she said. "Damage deposit plus first month's rent."

"Thank you," the woman said. "The previous tenant is leaving the day after Christmas. If I can arrange for the carpet cleaners that week you should be able to move in by New Year's Eve if you like."

"Great. Please let me know." Jenna shook hands with the older woman, whose oversized glasses magnified her eyes in an unsettling way, as though viewed from underwater, and left the rental office. As she walked along the shoveled path, she exhaled a shaky breath. This was a big step; she hadn't lived alone in a long time. Matt had already left for his fly-in job by the time she'd returned from the cabin, so knew nothing of her intentions. Though they'd guessed at it, the boys did not know her plans for certain. With a nervous laugh, Jenna realized even she hadn't known her plans until pulling out her chequebook five minutes ago.

When she reached the parking lot, she glanced back at the low-rise apartment building that was soon to be her home. It was decent; clean and spacious and in a good neighbourhood not far from her house and therefore her children. It even came partially furnished, something quite uncommon these days. As dusk fell, the outdoor lighting switched on and illuminated the well-kept exterior of the building. A light snow began to fall, the tiny balls of ice swirling aimlessly under the beams of light from each lamp. It reminded Jenna of the days spent at Whiteridge. It seemed miles away yet yesterday at the same time.

Surreal, subzero days had literally frozen time; created a bright, white universe with only her and Brandon to occupy it. She'd have given anything to stay in that suspended reality until the end of time, yet time was now her enemy. Learning of his illness had shaken her to the core, and brought everything into sharp focus. Not only how deeply she felt for him, but how things done in the darkness must always come to light.

She hadn't heard from Brandon since returning home from the resort. There were only two rehearsals left; one tomorrow and again on Thursday. She must tell him everything, lay every card on the table, and gamble that he would not choose the easy path; not stay his course and choose unhappiness only because it was less complicated, less messy, than striving for the real thing. But dammit, what else mattered? At this stage of life, when you've paid your dues, bought the dream house, raised your kids; what else fucking mattered but your own happiness?

Jenna shuddered, steeling herself against the cold, her frustration and her fears as she popped the Lexus's's door locks and slid behind the wheel. For better or worse, she'd already made her choice. Only Brandon could make his.

Chapter Ten

Roschkov scratched notes in the chart. The old man's wheezing breath became annoying as Brandon waited for the doctor to speak. *Get on with it, man. What's your verdict?*

The doctor looked up over wireframe lenses that perched near the end of his hooked nose. "The painful ejaculation you describe is concerning, but it is usually accompanied by much worse symptoms. That is encouraging. The best success for early treatment is anti-androgen medications. There are several forms, typically administered by injection."

Brandon nodded. "Which do you recommend? I have to return to Edmonton by tomorrow."

Roschkov closed the chart and set it aside. "We can start with a low dose of anti-androgens. Several brand names but the effect is the same."

"What's the effect?"

"Basically, anti-androgens suppress testosterone levels so that the cancer cells do not grow."

Brandon swallowed hard. Low testosterone didn't sound like a desirable condition. "How does it work?"

The old guy nearly cracked a smile. "Initially, it over-stimulates the glands, causing them to shut down production. This generally decreases libido, but you may get a rush of..." Roschkov paused and tipped his white-haired head side to side. "...boogie juice, to begin with. Your wife might be pleased."

Brandon held back the urge to laugh aloud. Behind his curmudgeonly demeanour, the Doc actually had a sense of humour. "Then what?"

"You may feel worse for the first while. But if we're lucky, the lesion will shrink and possibly disappear altogether."

"And if we're not lucky?"

Roschkov looked thoughtful for a moment. "Don't go to Las Vegas. The odds may not be in your favor."

Shit. He'd never been a gambling man, but had to believe Lady Luck would stand beside him at this particular game table. Just this once. She had to; he'd never asked her for any favors before. Surely she owed him. "Right. Let's get to it, then."

*

Jenna began packing in anticipation of moving out. Since she didn't plan on taking any furniture, she hoped to gather only what she needed for the immediate future as quickly and quietly as possible. With open suitcases gaping at her like hungry pelicans, she set her flute case and music folder aside for the day's rehearsal and sifted through her dresser drawers one by one.

Pieces of clothing that didn't make the cut went into a waiting garbage bag destined for the local charity drop off. Long overdue, the task became both cathartic and gut-wrenching, for buried at the bottom of one drawer lay an item she hadn't seen in a long time. A plastic case filled with family medical records; immunization cards, birth certificates, slips of paper that listed the boys' time of birth, gender, length, weight, and blood type. The damning evidence; the burden of proof that had lain hidden for so long.

Alongside were other, more sentimental items, like the hospital bracelets from when the boys were born, and a lock of their hair at about five or six months of age. She placed the case in a side pocket of one suitcase and zipped it shut.

Across the room, her cellphone uttered several tones. Jenna recognized each of them as either texts or emails to different inboxes. Grabbing the phone she thumbed the screen, startled to find an email from Ruby Smythe. She sucked in a breath at the subject line: REHEARSAL CANCELLED – TODAY, TUESDAY DECEMBER 10. She opened the message in alarm.

> *Hello members, please be advised that
> today's rehearsal has been cancelled.
> Mr. Marsh has unavoidable business to
> attend in Vancouver and will return late
> Wednesday. Dress Rehearsal will resume
> as scheduled on Thursday, December
> 12. Thank you, Ruby.*

Gone to Vancouver? He'd said he would likely return there for a few days during the season but hadn't mentioned it up at the cabin. Irrational fear swelled in her chest. Had she chased him away with her true confessions? Had his illness taken a turn for the worse? Had she caused it? Her mind swirled in a thousand worried scenarios, and with a pang of irony it struck her that Ruby Smythe knew of his whereabouts before she did.

Such a petty thing against all the other frightening possibilities, ludicrous that being caught unaware and uninformed brought her the most distress, but the thought of him in pain and alone overcame this fear. She scrolled through her phone logs until she found Brandon's number.

Voicemail kicked in on the fourth ring. "...You've reached Brandon Marsh..." *Damn.* Jenna didn't want to sound like she was keeping tabs on him, but this was too important. She must know. At the message prompt, she said simply, "Brand, its Jen. Are you alright? Please call me when you can." She stabbed the end call button with her finger, feeling frustrated and helpless. *Please let him be alright.*

Jenna abandoned her half-filled luggage and sat down to practice her music. Cancelling group rehearsal didn't mean they could slack off. The show must go on, as the old saying went; and the Winter Symphony would still debut on Saturday, December 14; only four days away.

Playing her flute gave her peace, and even though the melodic lines of her Winter Symphony parts painfully reminded her of Brandon, the exercise of playing the instrument both calmed her and renewed her outlook. Music had always been a refuge, an ever-present source of solace and strength. It had the power to evoke emotions both joyous and sad, to hurt and to heal. The doctor of the human soul.

She always knew that music would rescue her, no matter what hardships or challenges she would face, and she felt so now, as the air from her lungs channeled through the instrument. Without the musician, an instrument was merely wood and metal, valves and pads. The player made it come alive.

The strains and melodies of the Winter Symphony Overture rang through the room. Jenna lingered on the high notes, filling them with passion and vibrato, and cascaded through rapid runs both descending and ascending that resolved in quivering trills. Soft delicate cadences balanced against shrill staccato, forte one moment and pianissimo the next. When she stopped, her heart pounded with exhilaration. She would never give up her music.

Uplifted, and with a new sense of clarity, Jenna went downstairs to start dinner. Tonight she would tell the boys her plan, and though she would be leaving this house forever, had a feeling this Christmas with her sons would be something special.

*

The rehearsal stage seethed with motion. Orchestra members moved about setting chairs and stands. Pleasant chatter floated through the air along with the sounds of practice scales and snippets of Winter Symphony passages. The familiar, gentle cacophony made Jenna smile as she walked to her place in the front row and settled in the chair next to Heather.

Heather arranged her music on her stand. "Hi," she said. "Is Brandon back?"

Jenna shrugged nonchalantly, as though she hadn't already been casting around for a glimpse of him. Her pulse quickened when she spotted him approaching the podium. He looked tired, but he was here. A sigh of relief left her lips.

"All right guys," Brandon announced. "Almost show time. My apologies for skipping out on you, my bad. We may have to work extra hard today, but I know you're up to it." To Jenna's surprise, he produced a pair of reading glasses from his pocket. He gazed into the front row and flashed her a weak grin before slipping them on. Jenna smiled at this new look. Behind the black-rimmed lenses he appeared every bit the celebrated conductor he'd always wanted to be.

The group ran straight through all the movements of the Winter Symphony in order, as this would be the last rehearsal before the actual performance. When they finished the last piece, Brandon smiled and set down his baton.

"I think my work is done here," he said. He removed the glasses and looked out across the group. "You're ready. It's been a pleasure working with you all. Thank you. See you Saturday."

His words sounded so final Jenna's heart flinched. Did this exit speech include her? It felt wrong. She needed to talk to him before they all dispersed; tell him her news.

He stepped down off the podium and moved quickly off-stage. Jenna fumbled with her flute to return it to its case as fast as possible but the parts suddenly felt foreign and clumsy in her hands. She set the half-disassembled pieces down on her chair and followed in the direction Brandon had gone.

She spotted him in the wings near the sound technician's alcove and lengthened her stride to reach him. The sound of her heels on the hardwood stage echoed into the auditorium, causing him and the people gathered around him to look up. Jenna stopped short as they all about-faced. A tall woman with cropped red hair, dressed in mannish-styled slacks and jacket stood next to Brandon. The woman scanned Jenna up and down in curiosity.

"Jenna," Brandon said. "Great solo today."

"Thanks," Jenna said. "Can we talk for a minute?"

"Um, sure," he said, touching the redhead on her arm. "Excuse me for a sec," he said to her. He moved closer to

Jenna. "Sorry I didn't call you. I did get your message. In between appointments and the airport I just didn't get a chance."

Jenna glanced between him and the redhead. "Are you okay? What's going on? I was so worried...your illness..."

He waved a hand to stop her. "I went to see my doctor in Vancouver. It's alright, I decided to go ahead with the drug treatment. The shot slowed me down a bit, but in the long run its' the right thing to do. I won't need another injection for two weeks, so I can wrap things up here."

Jenna blinked, but kept eye contact. She could feel her guts starting to churn. "Wrap things up? And then what?"

Brandon smiled and placed a finger under her chin, tilting her face toward him. "It's been wonderful seeing you again. But I need to go home, deal with this." At her crestfallen expression he leaned in closer. "I have so much to live for," he said.

Now Jenna was more confused than ever. Was he referring to their relationship, his career, what? "How long before you'll be back?" Her eyes flicked back and forth across his face. She almost dreaded the answer.

"Not sure. There's a few issues that need resolving."

"Brandon?" A voice called from a few feet away. Jenna glanced sideways to see the redheaded woman gesturing his way.

"Is that one of the issues?" Jenna asked, her face growing hot.

Brandon remained expressionless. "You don't recognize her? I guess we've all changed quite a bit over the years, but..."

"No," she cut him off. "Should I?"

He shrugged and tilted his head in the woman's direction. "That's Trish."

Chapter Eleven

Jenna had never heard applause as loud and long as the response they received from the audience at the end of the Winter Symphony. The evening went perfectly. The musicians played at their highest level; the guest performers were stellar. The auditorium atmosphere was festive and sparkling. She could not have asked for a better capper to the holiday season than this fantastic concert.

Taylor and Kyle were in the audience, as always. They were Jenna's biggest fans and had attended every performance since they were old enough to sit solo in a theatre chair. Of course their dad had to accompany them in the early days, but Matt hadn't been to even one of her concerts in several years. The boys met her in the lobby all smiles. They looked so handsome in their dress clothes. "So what'd you guys think?"

"Bravo, Mom! Great concert." Taylor said.

"You look so beautiful, Mom," Kyle added, giving her a hug. "I love your hair. Let's go out for dinner to celebrate!"

Jenna smiled at both of them. "Thank you, honey." She'd worn her blond locks in an up-do for the performance, showing off glittering drop earrings. One long strand of hair hung in a loose ringlet against her cheek. Her classic and flattering black dress flowed to the floor. She spun around to send the skirt flaring out. "Yes, lets. Where shall we go? Kelsey's for wings?"

"You know it," Taylor said, pulling his truck keys from his pocket and steering them toward the main exit. As they moved toward the massive glass doors, Jenna saw Brandon leaving the hall side by side with Trish. She summoned the armour coating to form around her heart as she watched them disappear.

There'd been no promises, no plans; why did she feel so betrayed? She chastised herself mentally. It had been her idea all along to invite him to the cabin; her idea to seduce him and re-ignite an old flame. Hell, until Brandon told her otherwise she'd thought he was still married at the time. She had no 'right' to feel 'wronged'. A laugh escaped her mouth at the sick pun.

"What's so funny?" Kyle asked.

Jenna shook her head. "Nothing. Just feeling a little Christmas Crazy, you know?"

The boys smiled and nodded as Taylor held the doors for them to leave the concert hall.

*

Sounds from the kitchen woke her. Jenna's eyes fluttered open and she turned her head to the bedside clock. Christmas morning, and her guys were awake at 7:00 a.m.? That hadn't happened since they were five years old. A delicious excitement filled her; a very special Christmas indeed. Did she smell coffee already?

She shrugged on her white bathrobe that had seen better days and crept out into the hallway. She heard murmuring voices and the clink of coffee spoons against porcelain. She hoped they hadn't been into the presents without her! She still filled their Christmas stockings in spite of their ages—one of her guilty "mom" pleasures she refused to let go of.

She descended the stairs unseen until reaching the bottom few steps. "Merry Christmas!" she called.

"Merry Christmas," she heard in reply. For a second it sounded like three voices. She landed at the foot of the stairs and peeked around into the kitchen. Her smile froze solid on her face.

Matt Brophy sat at the kitchen bar with Taylor and Kyle beside him. "Surprise," Taylor said. "Look who's here."

"Hello Jenna." Matt looked at her with his cold blue gaze she'd come to know well.

Kyle stood and grabbed a mug from the counter. "Coffee, mom? With Kahlua?"

"Sure, thanks." She stepped cautiously into the kitchen. "What's going on here?"

"Looks like we're having a family Christmas morning to me," Matt said.

Jenna wrapped her robe more closely around her. "Looks that way," she agreed. "I thought you were working through Christmas?"

Matt sipped his coffee. "Weather turned bad, so the operation shut down for a few days. Gave guys the time off to visit family."

"You didn't call."

Taylor piped up. "He called me, Mom. We decided to keep it a surprise." He smiled, as though hoping to ease the tension meter down with his innocent grin. "You're surprised, right?"

Jenna let go of the breath she didn't realize she held. *What the hell.* It was Christmas morning and no time to get in a mood. "Sure am," she said, accepting the mug of coffee from Kyle and raising it in a toast. "Who wants to open gifts?"

The boys moved into the living room and sat down near the giant tree they'd decorated for her benefit. "Tay, put on some music," she called after them. Matt hung back in the kitchen. Jenna took a swig of coffee, wrestling with what to say to her husband whom she'd decided to leave by the end of the week. "I didn't get you a gift," she finally said.

"That's okay," Matt said as he rinsed his mug in the sink. "I got you one."

Jenna's radar went up. A gift? He'd been away for two weeks and they'd been fighting just before that. She'd even told him it was over. When would he have bought a gift? Why? "What is it?"

"Well, it's not one I could wrap exactly," he said, turning to face her.

She noticed dark hollows beneath his eyes. Camp life usually took a toll on most workers, but he looked extra-exhausted. *Served him right.*

"I booked us a trip. How would you like to spend New Year's Eve in Times Square?"

Jenna gaped at him. "Times Square? As in New York City?"

He folded his arms and cocked his head in mild annoyance. "Yeah, New York City. How many Times Squares do you know?" Even at his most generous he could still be a sarcastic asshole.

She stood there like a statue, still holding her coffee mug. He'd taken her completely by surprise, and not in a good way. It smacked of ulterior motives. "I...I don't know what to say," she stammered.

He crossed over to where she stood and kissed her on the cheek. "You might try thank you," he said. "And by the way, we also have tickets to *Elf the Musical* while we're there."

Before Jenna could speak, he turned away and walked into the living room.

"Mom, c'mon," she heard Kyle call.

"Coming," she said, her mind still in suspect mode. *Now?* She thought. After all these years of indifference to her love of music, now he came up with the trip of her dreams? It defied all things both natural and holy, and came at the worst possible time.

She followed him into the living room where the three men gathered around the tree. Christmas carols emanated from the TV tuned to one of the cheesy fireplace channels. The boys tore into their gifts as Matt looked on. Jenna stared at the scene. Her family sat right in front of her, complete and whole, and together on the most wonderful day of the year.

Suddenly, the preceding weeks seemed almost like a movie that had come to an end, and the credits were rolling. Real life displayed before her eyes. Had she made a mistake? Panic struck her as she recalled her recent actions. She'd gambled on the hope of a new life with an old love; and the odds didn't look good at this point. The vision of Brandon and his wife walking out the doors together after the Winter Symphony flashed in her brain and rebounded in her stomach with a sickening thud. Perhaps what she saw before her now was all that she was meant to have. Perhaps it was selfish to want more.

"Open this one," Taylor said, handing her a slim, square package.

She unwrapped the bright patterned paper to reveal a Michael Bublé Christmas Collection CD. "Oh Tay, I love it! Thank you." She gave him a smile and a kiss and watched them dive back into the pile of gifts. In all the excitement, they hadn't eaten anything yet. Jenna slipped into the kitchen to put the breakfast casserole she'd made the night before in the oven, then hurried upstairs to get dressed. She pulled her camera out of one of the bags she'd already packed. It seemed a good occasion to capture—her last Christmas in this house.

She took photos of the boys and Matt gathering and bagging the discarded wrappings. They each posed with their presents in front of the tree. Taylor held up a licensed NFL jersey from his favorite team. "Mom, do you know what Dad got me?" he said.

She lowered her camera. "Aren't you holding it?"

"No, this is from Kyle." He and Matt exchanged looks. Kyle grabbed one of the garbage bags and took it out to the garage, leaving the three of them alone in the living room.

Jenna shrugged her shoulders. "What?"

"A house," Taylor beamed. "When I turn 21, I get Aunt Leila's house!"

Jenna looked between them, then focused on Matt. "Your sister Leila's house? Where's Leila? When did this happen?"

"She wanted to retire in Mexico, so she sold me her house at a "family" price. She didn't need it so offered it to me. Now I'm giving it to Taylor."

"He's barely started college," Jenna sputtered. "What's he going to do with a house?"

"Think of it as a graduation present, not just a Christmas present," Matt said.

"What did you give Kyle?" Jenna asked, her anger rising. She hadn't heard anything about Leila selling her house. Family price or not, they couldn't afford another mortgage. What was he thinking? Once again he'd made a major decision without consulting her, or considering anyone else. "Does Kyle get a house, too? Or some other property I don't know about?"

Matt looked at her blankly. "No. Kyle's still a kid. There's no other property...what the hell are you talking about?"

"Uh, I'd better help Kyle," Taylor said, removing himself from the line of fire between them and grabbing the remaining garbage bag on his way out. Jenna felt bad having to start an argument in front of her son, especially when it involved him, but this was a major fuck-up.

"What is going on?" she demanded. "Trips to New York? Houses? You were the one complaining we needed cash. Where is this money coming from?"

"Well, I thought about what you said. We do have two paychecks coming in. I saw a good opportunity and I took it. As for New York..." he paused and looked down at the floor, avoiding eye contact. "I didn't like that you said I was boring. Thought maybe I could prove you wrong. Did you really mean it when you said you don't want to live with me anymore?"

There it was. An open door to the path she'd turned away from. In his own way, Jenna knew that Matt was trying to apologize. A tiny crack of compassion opened inside her, but she forced it shut. Did he not think her capable of knowing her own mind or making her own decisions? *He didn't like that I called him boring.* As usual, his actions were about himself and how he felt; not her at all. The familiar veil of anger began to cloud her vision once more.

"Yes I did. I'm moving out at the end of the week." He seemed stunned as he glared back at her. "So we can't be buying extra houses. My paycheck is spoken for."

Matt rose from the hassock he'd been sitting on by the tree and moved toward her. His expression turned from shocked to menacing. He gripped her roughly by the arm. "Fine," he hissed in her ear. "Move out. I don't need your permission or your paycheck. I can still buy a house for my son."

In all the years they'd been together, she'd never been afraid of him. Physical violence had never entered the picture, but her fear mounted now as the pressure of his fingers increased. The sick feeling of having gone too far rose in her throat again. "Then give it to Kyle," she gasped.

Matt's eyes narrowed. "What? Why not Taylor?"

Jenna felt certain there would be bruising on her arm as his fist tightened. "Because he's not your son."

Chapter Twelve

"I must admit, I've never seen anything like it," Roschkov said.

"You're certain?" Brandon asked. "Are there more test results to come back?"

"No; it's quite amazing. I should think your case will be in the next textbooks. Complete recovery after a single dose of anti-androgens. The growth has disappeared completely."

Brandon could barely believe it. Lady Luck had done more than stand beside him; she'd fixed the game. "That's good news, Doc. Great news."

"I suspect your self-care, that is, your diet and supplements prior to the injection, helped considerably," Roschkov commented.

"One question," Brandon said. "Will my glands jump-start again? Will the testosterone levels eventually return to normal?"

Roschkov chuckled. "They should. Given your age Brandon, I'm surprised you are worried about that. Ordinarily, men's bodies produce less and less testosterone as they age. Believe me, I know. Why? Is your wife anxious?"

"I don't have a wife, Doc. Two were enough for me." Brandon disconnected the call and drew a long breath. He'd been given another chance, in more ways than one. He looked down at the papers on the table in front of him. Just a few more tasks to perform and he'd be free.

When Trish came crawling back to town looking for a place to live with her new girlfriend, he'd been only too happy to negotiate a buy-out of their Vancouver house. She'd insisted on tagging along to the Winter Symphony concert to make sure he didn't change his mind. Property values had skyrocketed in the city and he'd netted a fair chunk of her change. He was done with this wet, gray town on BC's rocky coast. Alberta sunshine suited him much better and he could only hope this lucky streak held out when he got there.

With bold strokes he signed his name to the purchase offer and shed his old life like a lizard's worn skin.

*

"Thanks for helping me, Tay. I'm sure you have better plans for New Year's Eve than this." Jenna held the door as Taylor trudged in with a massive cardboard box in his arms.

"No problem. What you got in here, Mom…bricks?" Taylor grunted as he bent to set the box down. He let it drop the last few inches to the floor.

Jenna winced. "If I did, they'd be broken just now," she said with a chuckle. "Nope, just books and sheet music."

"Figures," he said, dusting his hands and glancing around her new apartment. "Nice place. Kinda small, though isn't it? After living in such a big house?"

Jenna shrugged. "Big house, big problems. How much space does one person really need?"

Taylor nodded. "I guess. One person and her flute. Are you sure about all this? It just seems—unreal somehow—you leaving home. I know you and dad are splitting, but it was your house too. Why should you leave? Why not him? Why not share it? Draw a chalk line down the middle or something."

"Yes, it was my house too," Jenna conceded with a nod. "But one of us had to take a huge step, and I knew it wouldn't be him. He's too stubborn." Jenna looked down at the box thoughtfully. "A chalk line," she smirked. "No, that wouldn't work. If I'd stayed much longer, the only chalk line might have been an outline on the carpet around one of our dead bodies."

"Geez, Mom. You have the darkest sense of humor sometimes."

"Sorry," she said with a laugh. "Here's an extra key. Can you get the last load of stuff from the house? I have to stop by the bank, then I'll pick up a pizza for us and meet you back here. Deal?"

"Only if it includes beer with that pizza," he replied, pocketing the key.

"Done." Jenna shouldered her purse and looked at her son. "I'm sorry about making a scene at Christmas. Hope it didn't ruin your surprise gift."

Taylor brushed his brown bangs away from his eyes and cocked his chin in a "no worries" gesture. "Nah. I'm not sure what I'm going to do with a house. Maybe I should rent it to you," he added as the thought struck him. "Then you wouldn't have to live in this tiny place, paying rent to people you don't know."

Jenna's eyes widened in amusement at his reasoning. "That's a smart thought Tay, thanks. But no, I wouldn't want the memories; nor the idea of being thankful to certain people."

"Why were you so upset about it?" Taylor asked. "Sounds like Dad got it for a steal."

"It wasn't that. He just...does things without consulting me. That's not what a marriage is supposed to be about. He assumed I'd agree, and that we would both finance it. Like I told him," she waved her arm across the space in which they stood. "My paycheck is spoken for."

Taylor zipped his jacket as he prepared to return outside. "It was more than the money though, wasn't it?"

Jenna smiled wistfully. The truth jumped up and down in her head, waving both hands like a keener student at the back of the class, desperate to be heard. "I can't really talk about it right now. Someday." She rubbed his arm. "So what do you want on your pizza?" she asked, changing the subject.

*

"Thanks Ruby. For everything." Brandon disconnected the call and pocketed his cell phone. As he pulled away from the gas station, the cloud cover he'd been driving under for hours suddenly broke. Beams of afternoon winter sunlight struck the mountainsides, lighting them in streaks of gold as he rejoined the main highway. A road sign in the distance grew larger as he approached. '*Welcome to Alberta*'. Brandon smiled. It seemed Lady Luck had taken a ride-a-long.

Dusk had fallen by the time he reached the Edmonton city limits. The car's GPS guided him to the address Ruby had somewhat reluctantly given him. But he insisted on getting this information in exchange for agreeing to her request. She could hardly have said no.

He pulled up in front of an impressive two-storey house in a new subdivision that hadn't even existed the last time he'd lived here. He let out a low whistle at the sight of the handsome stone facade and the picture-perfect holiday decor in the front yard. A private winter wonderland twinkled in multicolored merriment, complete with decorated trees, lighted garland scalloping over the veranda railing and a giant frosted holly wreath hanging on the brightly-painted front door. He didn't doubt that all of it was the product of Jenna's creativity. One of the many things he realized he loved about her.

With a pang of regret, it occurred to him how good she had it. He pondered whether he himself would have been able to provide such a beautiful home for her and two healthy boys. She'd said it was over, that she didn't want to be with her husband any more, but people say lots of things. Things they think they mean, but take it back in the cold light of reality.

In his experience, when push came to shove it was human nature to take the path of least resistance. Why would she even want to give up any of this, the nice house, the fancy cars, a secure financial situation? Hell, maybe they even had a family dog or two. More than one couple had co-existed in a stale, dead relationship for far less reason.

He turned off the ignition and got out of the car. Lights were on inside the house, so he made his way up the shoveled walk, the tidily swept veranda steps, and rang the doorbell. No dogs barked, and no immediate motion stirred inside. He stepped back from the door, waited a few moments longer. Being New Years Eve, he supposed that not a lot of people might be at home. As he turned to retrace his steps to the car, the door opened.

A work-hardened face greeted him, a man looking as though he'd seen some rough times and cold temperatures.

He stood in the open doorway, his posture somewhat hunched and a look of suspicion in his blue eyes. "Yes?"

"Hello, I'm looking for Jenna Layton?"

"You mean Brophy. Jenna Brophy," the man corrected him. "That's my wife. She hasn't been Layton for a long time. You a friend of hers?"

"Yes, I..." Brandon started. Hmmm. How should he put this? "Yes. An old friend. Is she here?"

"No." The man looked him up and down. "You look familiar. Have we met?"

Brandon shrugged. "Brandon Marsh," he said, extending a handshake. "I'm a musician friend of Jenna's. Perhaps we met at a concert a long time ago?"

"Matt Brophy," the man said, returning the handshake after what seemed a moment of indecision. "No, that's not it. Maybe I'm mistaken."

Brandon gave a noncommittal nod. "Well, when do you expect her back? I could stop by again later," he said, already retreating from the porch steps.

"She's not coming back. Sorry." With that, he closed the door. Brandon heard the deadbolt lock into place.

What the hell? Not coming back. Jenna really had meant what she'd said. But where did she go? The 'husband' didn't give much indication that he cared either way, and Brandon doubted if he'd reveal her location even if he asked. The guy seemed every bit the dick he'd suspected he would be. Jenna was right to leave him. No amount of money or security was worth sacrificing your own happiness.

Disappointed, he got back inside his car. He'd wanted to surprise her, but not knowing her whereabouts made that a bit difficult. He should call her; it wouldn't be as dramatic, but the logical thing to do. He pulled out his cell phone when it occurred to him that she might not answer...or that she wouldn't even want to talk to him after two weeks had gone by without contact. She certainly hadn't looked happy when she'd come face to face with Trish back at the concert hall.

God, he was a shit. Why did he never say what he meant, or do what he should when it came to Jenna? It was happening all over again, letting her get away without committing to anything or giving any kind of indication of his intentions. Letting doubt fill the void by being seen with his ex-wife, for fuck's sake. *Dumb-ass.*

He was about to punch in Jenna's number when motion outside caught his eye. A small truck coasted to a stop in front of the house, and a young man climbed out of the driver's seat. There was no mistaking the resemblance; clearly one of Jenna's boys. He watched the youth enter the house, and something cold took hold of Brandon's stomach. Jealousy? He got the eerie sensation that the house had swallowed the boy, taking with him the remains of a long-lost chance to have children of his own. He'd loved Jason and Mandy, no question. But the idea that what lay here, now, in front of his eyes was a life he could have had, should have had, filled his mind.

The sudden flood of thought weighed him down in his seat, his limbs seeming too heavy to move. Minutes passed; he didn't know how many. The front door opened again, and the young man emerged carrying a few cardboard boxes. He placed them in the back of his truck and returned to the house, bringing out an armload of loose items a moment later. Among them was a folding music stand. As he arranged them in the truck, Brandon's body snapped to life and got out of his car.

"Excuse me," he said, walking toward the kid.

The boy looked up from his task. "Hi," he said. "Can I help you?"

"My name's Brandon Marsh, I came to see Jenna Layton, uh, Brophy. I was told she isn't living here any more...would you know where I could find her?"

The young man sized him up for a moment. "Yeah, she moved out," he said finally. "I could let her know you're looking for her. You have a number, or a card or something?"

Smart kid. Brandon grinned sheepishly. He didn't own a business card. "I don't actually. It's okay, I think I have a number for her; I'll try that."

The boy closed the tailgate and moved to the driver's side. "Did you say Marsh?"

He'd' planned to meet Jenna's children sooner or later, so why not now? "Yeah, Brandon Marsh," he said. "And you are?"

"Taylor," he answered, his hazel-brown eyes widening in what seemed like recognition. "Jenna's my mom. Hey, you're that conductor guy. I remember your name on the programme. My mom plays in that group, is that where you know her from?"

"Yeah, we've known each other a long time, actually."

"Cool. Well, I gotta get going. I'll tell her you were here. Nice to meet you." Taylor climbed into the driver's seat of the truck and drove away.

It wasn't like Brandon to sneak around, but felt pretty certain if he followed the little truck it would lead him to Jenna. He could still call from outside when they got to wherever Taylor was going. His route led to a 3-storey walk-up apartment, the building's exterior lighting casting shadows on its walls as darkness fell. He watched the young man park in a visitor stall near the entrance and transport his various goods inside. Fifteen minutes passed without the boy returning. In another twenty minutes, he could make out a figure exiting the building and getting into the truck.

As the truck drove away, Brandon hit the call record for Jenna's cell phone. Her voicemail picked up after three rings. He disconnected and waited a few more minutes before retrying. Still no answer, but he listened to the sound of her voice greeting, a bittersweet emotion washing over him as it spoke. "Hi, you've reached Jenna. Leave a message or shoot me a text."

"Jenna, hi. It's Brandon. Sorry for not getting in touch over the last few weeks, been a little busy over the holidays. I...I've been thinking about you, and I've got some good news. Gimme a shout back, please. I miss you. Happy New Year." He stabbed the end call button, hoping his words were enough to make her at least call back. He'd try one more time before leaving; if she didn't return his call, he'd have to get a hotel room for the night, which might be a bit of a trick on New Year's Eve.

With a sigh, he re-started the engine to keep warm. If only keeping his relationship with the most important person in his life warm were as easy as turning a key. Perhaps he'd let the machinery grow too cold to start up again; seized with the stupidity of his own neglect. *C'mon Lady Luck. You've brought me this far. Don't bail on me now.*

Chapter Thirteen

"Mmmm, that was great," Taylor said, snatching the last slice before closing the cardboard lid of the takeout pizza box. "I was hungry."

"You, hungry? There's a shocker," Jenna said with a smile. "Just a small reward for your help. Ate it in record time, too. Oh, wait." She dug into her jean pocket and handed him a twenty. "For the gas."

"Thanks, Mom. You know I'll help you with anything you need, right? Anything. Just call me." He pulled out his wallet to tuck the bill inside.

"I know. You'll always be my Number One," she said, rising from the wooden table and chair set that had come with the place and taking their empty beer cans to the sink.

"Is that a Star Trek reference?" Taylor asked, biting into his pizza. "I never knew why you called me that."

Jenna laughed. "Kind of. You're sort of my First Officer, I suppose. Mostly it's exactly what it sounds like. You're my first child, my firstborn. You made me a Mom for the first time. No one else could ever be that, right?"

Taylor smiled. "Guess not. You didn't waste any time either. Dad said you guys spent your first anniversary with me in your arms. Is that true?"

Jenna leaned against the sink and nodded thoughtfully. "Yup. You were only a few months old. And no sooner had I put all the baby bottles away, we found out Kyle was on his way." She lifted her hands in the air. "Hey, I was over thirty already. Didn't have a lot of time to waste."

Taylor laughed and wiped his hands on a napkin. "Me neither. I have a party to get to." He stood as well, handing Jenna the empty pizza box. "You gonna be okay here all alone on New Year's Eve? Sounds kinda lonely."

"I have plenty to do," she said, gesturing at the stacks of boxes on the floor and piles of clothes draped over the squarish, faded sofa that had also been part of the rental agreement. The only furniture she'd brought was a new bedframe and mattress which still lay disassembled in the bedroom where the furniture store delivery guys had left it.

"Okay. Happy New Year, love ya," he said, giving her a hug and shrugging on his jacket.

"Bye, Tay." She closed the door behind her son and winced against the sting of tears building around her eyeballs. *Alone at last.* Isn't that what she wanted?

This isn't how I pictured my life turning out. She felt tired and grubby from the move. She went to her bedroom, ignoring the big, white, and conspicuously empty mattress lying on the floor. A nice hot shower would make her feel better, and hopefully ready to collapse into dreamless slumber before the clock struck midnight.

Jenna let the hot water rush over her. The comforting warmth of a shower always provided a little suspended time—precious minutes where the entire world consisted only of a tiny porcelain enclosure. A safe place where cares or concerns were not allowed to enter, and had the added benefit of shielding the sounds of hollow sobs while bawling one's head off.

Had she done the right thing? Yes. Had she hoped to live alone for the rest of her life? No. She'd risked everything she'd built in the last two decades on one last shot at the thing she'd always wanted—being truly, madly in love with the one person she could not forget.

But he wasn't here.

She twisted the taps shut, toweled off and slipped into her worn white bathrobe that encircled her like an old friend. She opened the bathroom door to let the steam escape as she combed through her long, wet hair. Switching off the fan, she heard her cell phone ringing in the bedroom. One of her boys calling, most likely. Her heart skipped a beat as she read the number on the screen.

"Brandon?" she answered, straining to hear over the blood pounding in her ears.

"Hi Jenna. Happy New Year."

She sank down onto the mattress still covered in plastic overwrap, feeling lightheaded. "H-Happy New Year to you... how was your Christmas?"

"Fine, good...I called earlier…did you get my message?"

"No...I was in the shower." Jenna struggled to quell the sensations rioting inside her. She felt dizzy, as though her heart sucked the blood away from every region of her body to sustain its frantic beating. Joy, hope and fear all cycled equally inside it. If Brandon was calling to say goodbye, he was a little late. His fortnight of silence conveyed the message louder than any words, and his hesitation now painfully underscored it.

"Can I come see you?" His voice sounded strained and doubtful. Like he expected her to say no. If he knew her at all, believed what she'd said to him all these weeks, he would know better. She turned her head away to draw in a shaky breath before speaking again.

"If you want to, of course. Are you planning a trip to the city?"

"Uh, yeah...no. Not really." He snickered nervously. "I'm already here. In fact, I think I'm right outside your door."

My door? How could he possibly know where she was? Unless...he'd been to the house. Oh, shit. That would not be good at all. "Um, I have a new address; I've just moved into a new place, and it's kind of a mess..."

"I know. It's a long story, but I'm outside an apartment building on 23rd and Rutherford, and if it's the right one, can I come up? Please?"

Jenna swallowed hard, and shivered as the beads of water dripped down her neck from her wet hair. He was not one for surprises; his history clearly leaned toward considered, calculated and deliberate actions. The easy path; one of least resistance. Who could have told him where she lived now? Something was not right here; something had changed; and for good or bad, she had to know. "Just press 304 when you get inside the doors."

"Thanks. I'll be right up."

Her hair couldn't be helped, and Jenna thought about exchanging her ratty robe for regular clothes, but knew that Brandon had seen her in a far less prepared state. He was here. He wanted to see her. Nothing else mattered. The intercom buzzed and she ran to unlock the outer door.

Her heart ticked the passing seconds until he knocked. He stood there in the hallway, looking tired and worn, but as dear and handsome to her as he'd ever been. The lines in his face seemed to illustrate their long journey together, a map to this moment. She held out her hand.

He took it and stepped across the threshold, into her arms and into her life—again. But was it just in passing? In farewell? A hello, or a goodbye? He held her close, his arms circling around her waist, one hand trailing up her back to cup the back of her head, wet strands of her hair curling over his fingers. "Jenna," he whispered, the sound caressing her ear as he spoke. "I'm so sorry."

She winced, squeezing her eyes shut as her arms went around his neck. They'd said 'sorry' to each other so many times the words had lost all meaning—become a caption for the wistful, impressionist painting of their lives. A representation rather than a portrait. Her gut went hollow at the phrase. "I know."

He moved his hands to frame her face, forcing her to meet his brown-sugar gaze. She could be lost so easily within it, and wanted nothing more than to do so at this moment. But it would only cause more pain.

He shook his head. "No, you don't. Not even close. I'm sorry for not calling you; for letting you think things that weren't true, for allowing that beautiful, creative mind of yours to fill in the blanks, improvise the missing bars on the page. I'm an idiot, and an arrogant asshole to think you'd give me another chance but, I'm asking for one. Will you give it to me?"

Her jaws still locked between his hands, Jenna wiggled a tiny nod. Damn her soul, she would. She'd give him every chance, just as she hoped medical science had given him.

"Thank you." Before he released his grip, he kissed her; a kiss filled not with raw passion, but things much more meaningful. Truth. Friendship. Promise.

"I've left Vancouver," he said. "I've sold the house, and I'm cancer free—the treatment worked like magic. Even my doc thought it was a miracle. I don't deserve a miracle, but if it is one, I know it's so that I can make things right. Make them the way it should be...should have been all along."

"That's…great news. I'm so happy for you," Jenna said, her voice choked with emotion. She didn't want to speak or think any further than that—that he was alright, and alive, and here.

"That's not all of it," he said, grinning. "I've been offered Winston's job. He's retiring. Ruby called me, and I told her I'd only take the job if she gave me your address; so that I could just turn up and surprise you. I guess the surprise was on me."

"You talked to my ex." Jenna grimaced. "Some surprise, huh?"

"It doesn't matter. It only matters that I found you, so that I can tell you in person."

"Tell me what, exactly?" she asked. *Say it. Spell it out. So we can't misunderstand this time.*

"What do you think?" he said, his brow wrinkling in exasperation. "That I want to be with you, if you'll still have me."

Jenna's body trembled. *For how long?* How long before illness returned to claim him? Before time and circumstances tore them apart again? It pained her to analyze it, even when she was hearing the words she'd longed for. But it had to be real; she had to be sure. There were no third chances. She swiped a strand of hair away from her face. "Are you certain it's what you want, really certain? I don't mean to disbelieve you, but there's so many things in our way; old ghosts, broken promises and dreams. Like you said, I don't want us to have any regrets."

"Oh, I have plenty of regrets," he sighed, gripping her by the shoulders. "I regret that I didn't see what you meant to me…that I didn't tie you to my bed that night to stop you from marrying that jerk. That I let twenty years pass without telling you how I felt. That I let you down, and let you go. But none of those compare to what I'd feel if I didn't try to win you back now…tell you that I love you, and I want to be with you for whatever time fate allows my sorry ass to have. I've never been more certain of anything, Jenna."

Fate. Miracles. Both had brought them to this moment, to the Finale in the symphony of their lives. Every note would be pure joy. "Then be with me," Jenna said, locking her eyes with his. "Starting right now."

Chapter Fourteen

She grabbed the lapels of his jacket and drew him further into the tiny apartment, claiming him with her kiss. Jenna tugged at the material until Brandon lowered his arms and shucked the jacket to the floor. When they reached the sofa she collapsed onto it, pulling him with her and landing them both atop its tweedy cushions. She wanted him now, right here, right now, while their promises to each other still echoed in the air.

She kissed his lips, his face, every piece of skin she could reach; the ridge of his shoulders, his Adam's apple and the little dip in his collarbone, exposing more as she peeled away his shirt and threw it to the carpet

He shoved aside the folds of her robe, cupping her breasts in his palms. Her nipples went taut, tingling to attention under his touch as his thumbs beaded over them. She untied the loose knot of her belt to free the rest of her body and lay back, opening herself to him completely.

His mouth moved over the blushing mound of her breast, sucking hard in between roving passes of his tongue over the tortured, swelling nipple. Jenna gasped inward, his ministrations sending shockwaves of pleasure down through her core to crest between her legs. His hand traversed a path across her ribs, around her hip and to the underside of her firm thigh. He raised her leg with a gentle push.

Her wet, throbbing pussy rubbed against his chest, slaking him with moisture as he writhed lower, trailing kisses down her quivering torso as he went. When he paused to circle his tongue in her navel, she nearly exploded in arousal, her body arching beneath him. He withdrew his tongue, the wetness left in her belly button evaporating in chills as he breathed over it. She looked down to see him grinning at her, the inside of her knee pressing against his cheek. "Whatever you're going to do, don't stop now," Jenna gasped.

He pushed her other knee upward and rested both of her feet on his muscled shoulders. Her molten-hot pussy lay open to him, and he nuzzled his face in its wet warmth. His murmured words floated up to her as she panted in blind ecstasy. "Gonna rock your world so hard, baby..."

His tongue parted her quivering pussy lips to reach the soft swollen nub of her clit, nudging it lovingly up and down. Her hands threaded into his dark hair laced with slivers of gray. "Finish me," she moaned, her knees shaking.

A sudden noise, barely heard over the thundering of her pulse and her ragged breaths, came from the direction of the door. The sound of the deadbolt unlocking. Brandon raised his head, withdrawing from her wanting flesh. Jenna moaned at such exquisite pleasure interrupted. Her gaze snapped to the door, clutching for the remnants of her robe as it opened.

"Hey mom, I forgot my wallet..." Taylor said as he breezed into the room, then froze in place with his hand still on the doorknob. He stared at them in shock as he dropped his arm and let it fall shut behind him.

"Taylor," Jenna cried, closing the material around herself. Brandon stood, shirtless but still otherwise clothed, and glared toward the door. "Taylor," she said again, at a loss for any words that could possibly matter in this situation. She could hardly scold him for not knocking. He had a key.

Her son had no words either, only a burning look of betrayal in his eyes. Her heart seemed to splash into her stomach, sending a hot backwash of shame and embarrassment upward. "Taylor, I'm...it's..."

"The reason you moved out?" he finished for her, gesturing toward Brandon.

"No, honey." She swallowed painfully and wrapped her robe tighter, helplessly searching for the dangling belt ends. Brandon stepped back and pulled on his shirt. "Tay, this is Brandon."

"Yeah I know who he is," he said, cutting her off. "Having a private recital with the Maestro, huh? Is that how you move up in the ranks?"

Taylor moved away toward the kitchen, where his wallet lay on the edge of the table. He'd taken it out when she gave him the gas money. "No, stop it. This isn't what you think."

"I don't have to think. I can see," he growled. His disapproval felt worse than being lashed with a whip.

"Listen to me." She turned toward Brandon. "Both of you." She swallowed hard. It was the worst scenario imaginable, but she had to tell them. "This isn't the way I wanted the two of you to meet, but...Brandon, this is Taylor; Taylor, this is Brandon Marsh. Your father."

Taylor turned slowly toward her, his eyes narrowed. "What?"

Brandon stood stock-still, his face stony. "I'm sorry," Jenna continued. "I wish the circumstances were...better...but it's the truth. "I'm sorry I never told you, either of you. Things were complicated, and it would have done more harm than good to bring it up before now."

"My father is Matt Brophy," Taylor said firmly. "Not some dude I just met today."

"Matt was your father in every way but one," Jenna said.

"Jenna," Brandon interrupted. "I think we should talk about this another time."

"When?" Jenna rounded on him. "After you've disappeared again? After our son drives away in anger and gets in an accident? No, we'll talk about it now."

"I'm leaving," Taylor said, marching toward the door.

"Taylor, wait. I know you're upset. Please don't drive while you feel this way."

Taylor paused and cast a sidelong glance at the two of them as they stood side by side. His gaze traveled up and down Brandon's height. "I don't know how I feel right now." He switched his sights onto his mother, then shook his head. "How could you...how could you do this to us? Me, Dad... and what about Kyle? Does he have a surprise father out there somewhere, too?"

Jenna's eyes misted over with tears. "No, no. I told you we spent our first anniversary with you in my arms. What happened between Brandon and me...was before I got married. I was never unfaithful to my husband. Matt is Kyle's father."

Taylor snorted. "Either way you're saying I have a half-brother. How do you think Kyle will react? You've hurt all of us, Mom. Him, too." Taylor jerked his chin toward Brandon. He twisted the door open. "I have to go."

The sound of it slamming struck Jenna's heart like a hammer blow. She pressed a hand to her chest, the pain every bit as real. Brandon's fingers curled inside the crook of her elbow and turned her to face him. His expression registered only shock and concern; not anger. "I understand you keeping it a secret from your family. And from me."

Jenna nodded weakly through her tears. Just words. Would anyone truly understand? Truly forgive? "He said you met…? How?"

"I was parked by your house when he drove up, and…he looked so much like you…I knew. I asked if he knew where you were. He didn't say." Brandon shook his head. "So I followed him. I had a hunch he'd lead me to you."

Jenna focused her blurry eyes on him. "He looks a lot like you, too," she said. "And he's right. I've hurt everyone, including you. I'm sorry."

"Including yourself," Brandon said, drawing her into his arms. "Stop apologizing. That can't have been easy, burying that information all those years. And what just happened… that was coincidence. You couldn't have stopped it."

"I know. I just…would have broken the news a little differently." She lifted her gaze to meet his. "Does this change any of what you said? I wouldn't blame you if it did…"

Brandon's hands moved from around her waist to take her face between his palms. "No," he said, interrupting her. "God, no. I have more reason than ever to be here. Get to know my son. If he'll let me." He shook his head in wonderment. "How? Did it happen? That night…you said…"

"I took a chance," she said. "I lied about being on the pill. It wasn't smart of me, but…I wanted that chance. I knew I could never have you, so I thought, if I take this chance, I might keep some piece of you with me forever." A sob escaped from deep within her lungs, as though finally setting free the painstakingly guarded secret she'd kept from the world for so long. She laid her cheek on his chest, felt the thrum of his heartbeat, and prayed for forgiveness.

"That was one hell of a chance," he murmured, stroking her now partially dry hair. "At that point, I'm pretty sure it was me who could never have you, Jenna. You got married practically the next day. You chose someone else."

"I chose someone else because I couldn't have you!" she sobbed. "You never gave me any indication you cared, or saw me as other than a friend since we left high school. You married Nina, you moved on. I was thirty years old. I wanted a husband, a family. Since you couldn't be the husband, I guess in my twisted way I thought you could provide the family." She wiggled her head against Brandon's shirt. "I didn't say it was logical."

Pained silence reigned for several moments, allowing all secrets, regrets and doubts to settle like snow atop them. Brandon finally spoke.

"Logic seldom applies when your heart is involved. When did you know…I mean, for sure…that Taylor was ours?" he asked.

"Blood tests don't lie. They have to type mothers and babies, to check for antigen compatibility. I'm an A. So is Taylor. Matt is type B."

Brandon nodded slowly. "Science doesn't lie. You could still have told me."

"It was my decision, my reckless, passion-soaked decision; why involve you in something that couldn't be changed? I didn't know how you'd react. Maybe you'd have resented me; resented the baby. And after he was born…you moved away. I heard you'd gotten married again. Game over."

His embrace tightened around her, crushing her against him. "It didn't have to be. I never had any children, natural children, of my own. I would have been thrilled. I *am* thrilled, Jenna; don't ever think otherwise."

"Looks like we can't say the same for Taylor," Jenna sighed. "I guess there was no good way to tell him."

"He'll come around…he's smart. Like his mother."

"Yeah, well, Mother's done some not so smart things. Crazy things."

"Maybe. But I'm crazy about her," Brandon said, easing his grip and raising her chin to look into her face. "You don't have the patent on crazy, trust me. I was crazy enough to let you go. Apparently crazy enough to make a woman switch teams," he chuckled without mirth. He leaned down and placed a warm kiss on her troubled lips. "I'll talk to him. He'll understand, eventually. If he wants to punch my lights out first, that's okay, too."

"He may not be ready to talk for awhile."

"I'm not going anywhere…unless…you'd rather I left?"

Jenna's head wobbled side to side, her hands fisting the material of his shirt. "You sold your house; taken on a new job; found your family. You've got nowhere else to go, mister.

Not this time." Still grasping his clothing, she led him to the unfurnished bedroom that couldn't be any more perfect than the royal suite of a palace. It had all it needed in two star-crossed souls coming together within it at last.

Chapter Fifteen

"Thanks for coming, Tay," Jenna said, sliding into the chair opposite her son. January sunlight streamed through the windows of the neighborhood coffee shop, made extra bright with the reflection off the snow outside. "I'm sorry if I ruined your New Year's; I wasn't trying to keep anything from you, or sneak around behind your back. I would have told you the next day, you know that, don't you?"

Taylor rubbed his palms against his steaming cup of coffee on the table between them. "You kept a secret for 19 years," he said solemnly. "Why not a few more? I could have lived happily never knowing it."

"Well, given the situation…it had to be said. Brandon didn't know, either. He found out the truth the same moment you did."

"He what?" Taylor said, his eyes widening beneath a furrowed brow. "You lied to him all these years too?"

"I never lied to anyone, Tay. Be fair. I just withheld the facts."

"What did you tell Dad?"

"I told Matt that he wasn't your father. I didn't say who was."

"And Kyle? Have you told him about me?"

Jenna shook her head. "Not yet. I don't know what Matt might have told him before he left again for work. I guess I'll need to see them both at the same time. Make sure everyone has the story straight. I don't want any false conclusions made about Kyle. Matt might take it out on him. Or you. I'd watch out for him for awhile…maybe keep your distance."

"I'm not afraid of him."

"I'm glad you've had no reason to be."

"Maybe he'll revoke my Christmas gift," Taylor scoffed.

"He won't. He's too damn stubborn for one thing," Jenna said, taking a sip from her own mug. "If you'd rather not be around him though, you can stay with me for awhile."

Taylor looked up. "What about the Maestro? Looked like he was planning on moving right in on the territory."

"His name is Brandon. And there are two bedrooms, you know."

Taylor rolled his eyes. "No thanks; that's just…no. Not happening. Too weird."

"I can understand that," Jenna smirked. "But please know that I would never shut you out because of him."

Taylor's brow wrinkled in puzzlement. "Why'd you do it, Mom? Why'd you marry Dad if you were in love with someone else?" He paused. "I assume you were in love. Or was I a mistake?"

His words felt like a punch to the gut. She'd made him question his entire existence by revealing the truth; the last thing she'd ever intended. How could she explain the warped workings of her heart, and still expect him to respect her and the decisions she'd made? He was young, too. He wouldn't be exempt from making decisions based on his emotions in the years to come. Her answer now could be one of the most important lessons she could offer. She looked her son in the eyes.

"Oh, Taylor; you weren't a mistake. Not ever. Yes I was in love; maybe too much, because at the time I loved both Matt and Brandon. Maybe I was even lucky in a way, to feel so deeply for more than one person. I know it's lame to say 'it's complicated' but it's the truth. You're a child of people who loved each other."

"How do you know he loved you? Brandon, that is." Taylor countered. "If he cared, wouldn't he have stood by you? By me?"

To Jenna, Taylor looked as if he felt more adrift and...yes, betrayed...than before. She shriveled inside; she was hurting more than helping. "He couldn't. I was getting married in a few days."

"Why didn't you marry him instead? Called off the wedding? People do that all the time."

Jenna shook her head. "It was too late. You don't understand. We hadn't seen each other in years. Brandon and I go way back; he was my first love, when I was really, really young. You know how that feels, don't you? That person you never forget, no matter how many years go by?"

Taylor shrugged, as though casting off an unpleasant memory. "Sort of."

"You're going to love a lot of people in your life, Tay. I have. I loved my parents. I love you and Kyle. I loved your Dad for a long time. And yes, I love Brandon too; luckily, he and I both have a chance to explore that now. If I've learned anything, if there's anything I can pass on to you that I know is true, it's that you can love more than one thing, one person, at a time. Equally. And that you should treasure them all. Embrace them, be loyal to them, but not regret them."

Taylor took in her words, his expression unreadable. He inhaled deeply and squared his shoulders. "I want you to be happy, mom. That's all. I know you haven't been happy for a long time. Will he make you happy?"

"He already does, Tay. More than you know."

Taylor's lower lip protruded. "How do you think he feels about me? He doesn't know me any more than I know him."

Jenna smiled. "Here's your chance to find out," she said, rising from her chair and gesturing off to one side. From across the room, Brandon strode toward them, looking apprehensive but dashing in a black wool overcoat that set off his silver-laced hair and close-trimmed beard that he'd grown over the past weeks. She'd asked him to come along; meet his son for the first, or perhaps second, time.

"Hello Taylor," Brandon said, extending a hand.

Taylor looked up in surprise, rising from his chair to accept the handshake. "Hello. Again." Jenna offered Brandon her seat and moved away, allowing her men to have this very important moment in private. They both sat and sized each other up.

"I apologize if I caused you any distress the other night," Brandon said. "I wasn't expecting anyone to..." he waved his hand in a helpless gesture.

"Me either," Taylor said, twisting his coffee stir stick between his fingers. "I should have knocked."

Brandon folded his arms across the table, eyeing his newly discovered son. "I hear you're studying engineering at University. Are you finding it interesting?" he asked.

Taylor shuffled his feet under the table and tossed the stir stick aside. "Look, we could make polite conversation all day, but I need to know some things first," he said, making eye contact.

"Sure," Brandon said, straightening.

"Do you love my mother? Did you ever love her?"

"Yes. To both questions."

"Did you ever want to marry her?"

Brandon's lips pursed, pondering the question that had multiple answers. "I didn't have the opportunity," he finally said.

"That doesn't answer my question. Did you ever ask her?"

"I didn't know she felt that way about me at that point in time. Our relationship was..."

"Don't say complicated," Taylor warned.

"Far-reaching," Brandon continued. "We'd known each other a long time. We dated. We broke up. There has always been unfinished business between us. We moved in different directions after school ended. We caught up once in awhile, and for a time when we found ourselves in the same orchestra. I was going through a divorce when we got together one night. A night that led to you, I've recently learned. And she invited me, by the way, to have sex that night." Taylor winced. "Sorry if I'm being too graphic," Brandon apologized. "She was already getting married to someone else. I wasn't exactly free, and wasn't about to blow up her wedding plans just because I'd come to a realization too late."

Brandon leaned forward again. "If the timing had been right, who knows how things would have turned out. If you're asking would I have wanted to marry her given the chance, then the answer is yes. But that chance was lost. It's history. What matters is what we do now."

Taylor met his level gaze. "I guess. Can't turn back the clock, can you."

"No. Sometimes you don't see things clearly until it's too late. But it's never too late to acknowledge them, to make reparations. To enjoy what's still here, right now, in the present. I hope this is one of those times, Taylor. Your mom and dad did a wonderful job raising you. I'd be proud to get to know the person you've become."

"My dad? You mean Matt Brophy."

Brandon nodded. "I meant your dad. That's not me. Not yet, anyway. I have to earn that."

"I don't need a dad anymore," Taylor said, shoving his empty cup aside as if to illustrate the point.

Brandon smiled ruefully. "No. I don't suppose you do. But will you take friend, for the moment?"

Taylor looked up, his jaw working back and forth in consideration of his answer. "If it makes my mother happy," he said. "You have to promise you'll make her happy. And keep her that way."

"I know you and I being friends will make her happy for a start," Brandon said, then nodded. "I promise. When you've been given a second chance, you make sure you don't miss." He held out his hand once more. "What do you say? Friends?"

Taylor cast a sideways glance toward Jenna, seated at a table across the room. "Yeah," he said, returning the handshake as though cementing a pact between them; a pact to bring unconditional happiness to the woman they both adored. "Friends. For now."

Brandon smiled in earnest. The first steps had begun in making the past, the present and the future a complete circle; the resolving chord in a symphony of lives bound together by love, fate and music.

Epilogue

December, one year later

The final notes soared into the heights of the concert hall, their fading echoes bringing the audience to their feet in a standing ovation. Such immediate and heartfelt response brought tears to Jenna's eyes. The New Edmonton North Shore Orchestra had poured their hearts into the performance and were rewarded with the best kind of compensation, the only kind that truly mattered to musicians; the appreciation of an audience emotionally moved by the music they'd played.

As she scanned the rows of applauding hands, the entire length of the hall as well as the balconies, her vision came to rest on someone who'd made it possible, made it special, as he stood at the front of the stage.

Conductor Brandon Marsh.

This year's programme, *Winter Symphony II*, topped even the premiere performance of the previous December, the score modified and enhanced by Brandon's expert vision, depth of musical and performance knowledge, and inspired leadership. He looked all at once handsome, distinguished and enraptured as he smiled in response, allowing the praise and applause to flood over him before taking a modest bow.

He stepped aside to acknowledge his performers with a sweep of his arm, eliciting even louder cheers from the crowd. Brandon himself applauded, signalling each of the soloists to stand and receive their accolades. Jenna stood as he pointed at her, happily accepting both the appreciation of the audience and the undisguised pride in his gaze, reserved just for her. It felt as close to flying as Jenna could imagine, her very soul seeming to take flight on wings of pure joy.

But she wasn't flying anywhere without the love of her life; the man who stood before the group now, reveling in their spectacular accomplishment and adding his praise to that of the patrons that filled the hall. The one person who'd been all she ever wanted, and everything she'd hoped for. Christmas was a time of wishes, gifts and miracles. Whether or not the season had anything to do with it, her own wishes had come true.

As the musicians filed off stage past their beaming conductor, Brandon took Jenna's hand and kissed it lightly. "Great job, babes."

"You too, Maestro," she said, squeezing his fingers as they curled beneath hers. She longed to touch him in many more ways, in every way; but that would have to wait until later. They had time. Christmas miracles or no, they'd received the greatest gifts of all. Love, and the time to share it.

As Jenna left the dressing room, flute case in hand, Taylor and Kyle were waiting for her. They looked sharp in their tailored suits, but nothing seemed as beautiful as the smiles on her son's faces. She felt so grateful to have their support and acceptance of her choices and of Brandon in her life; it had made the events of last year so much easier on everyone, from moving, to real estate transactions, and even divorce proceedings on two sides.

Her boys took it all in stride, and somewhere in the middle of it managed to build great relationships with both Matt and Brandon. In fact, they seemed to enjoy having two dads to learn from, spend guy time with, and only occasionally, disagree with. Families were made of relationships, not facts on paper.

"Fantastic performance, Mom!" Taylor said.

"I think it was even better than last year," Kyle added.

"It *was* better than last year," Jenna agreed. "For lots of reasons." She glanced off to the side as Brandon's tuxedoed figure approached. Both boys turned in the direction of her gaze.

"Bravo, Maestro," Taylor said as Brandon joined them. Jenna knew that Brandon's smile reflected more than his acceptance of a compliment; it held the satisfaction of receiving praise from his family. Something no audience applause would ever compare to.

"Thank you," Brandon said with a deferential nod to Taylor, his eyes sweeping across the three of them. "What'd you think, Kyle?"

"Awesome," Kyle answered. "Even better than last year. Might be because of the venue, though."

Jenna laughed. "Yeah, Carnegie Hall does rather make the Winspear Centre pale a bit."

"I can't believe we're standing here behind one of the most famous stages in the world," Taylor said.

"I can't believe we're standing in New York City," Kyle added, his arms thrown wide. "This is the most awesome Christmas vacation ever."

"Hey, some of us came here to work," Brandon teased.

"And some of us came for both," Jenna said, interlocking her arm with Brandon's. "Work's over for today. Time to enjoy our vacation."

"Yeah, we'd better get going if we want to make curtain for *Elf*," Taylor reminded them.

"Alright, alright. Mustn't bask in our glory for too long," Brandon chuckled in mock sarcasm. "We only just pulled off a musical miracle landing the New North Shore Orchestra a gig in the Big Apple."

"Yes, we know. All thanks to our brilliant new director," Jenna said, planting a kiss on Brandon's cheek. She wanted to kiss many other places, too; but again, that would have to wait for the privacy of their hotel room.

"So let's rock this town to celebrate," Taylor said, ushering them toward the exit. "I wanna see it all. Light it up like a Christmas Tree."

They left the concert hall and climbed into the waiting limo provided by the tour operators, who'd seen to every detail of the New York trip ever since Brandon received the invitation to perform at Carnegie six months into his first year as Director. It was a monumental achievement for any group, not to mention for a relatively unknown civic orchestra. The members were beyond thrilled with their new full-time conductor, and even more so to have been offered such an opportunity.

Jenna settled into the private rear seat next to Brandon while the boys rode up front to ensure they got the best view possible out the panoramic windows. "You are brilliant, you know," Jenna confirmed, leaning into him as she laid her head against his suited chest. "I don't think anyone else could have brought the North Shore to this level."

"Thanks, babes. Let's just say I was inspired to do better." He placed his arm around her shoulders and pulled her tighter to him. "Be better."

"You are better. Cancer free for an entire year," she reminded him. "And you made the Winter Symphony better than ever."

He tipped her face upward with a finger under her chin. "A minor achievement compared to everything else I've gained," he said. "My health, a gig I love. A son."

"Oh, is that all," Jenna teased.

"And you," he whispered, bending his head lower until their lips met. The kiss was simple, yet held so much; love, passion, but also hope, forgiveness, and the warmth of knowing they'd truly come home. Jenna knew she and Brandon would always be home as long as they were together. Home was in each other's hearts, not a place on a map. Happily however, the money from Brandon's Vancouver house bought them one nearly twice its size in a city like Edmonton, leaving cash to spare.

Their kiss ended, but their eyes lingered on each other's for a long moment before directing their attention outside. The traditional and always magnificent seventy-five foot Norway spruce glittered like a galaxy of stars in front of Rockefeller Center. "Now there's a Christmas tree," Kyle exclaimed.

"It's kind of like us, you know," Brandon said as they took in the sight.

"What, a giant Christmas tree?" Jenna laughed.

"No, the Winter Symphony; Winter in general, Christmas and New Year's. The whole thing is about looking back and honoring what's passed, but also forward to what's ahead."

Jenna smiled at the idea. It fit perfectly; the music of *Winter Symphony II* was the ideal accompaniment to the story of their lives together. It contained many complex movements, some uplifting, some nostalgic, some sorrowful; but the joyous grand finale was still ongoing. "Hmm, sounds like more unfinished business to me," she chuckled softly.

Brandon joined in her laughter, encircling her with both arms. "I hope we never finish," he whispered, his wonderfully gray, respectable-looking and expertly trimmed Vandyke beard tickling her ear. "Because our business together is just too much fun."

The End

Other titles by Jean Maxwell:

The Witch Doctor
Nine Lives Chronicles - Book One

Indecent Proposal
Workplace Gone Wild - Book One

El Mirador
Spanish Seduction - Book One

El Precio: The Price of Passion
Spanish Seduction - Book Two

COMING SOON:

Incendio
Spanish Seduction - Book Three